SPACE INVADERS

KATHY LEE

© Kathy Lee 2011
First published 2011
ISBN 978 1 84427 507 6

Scripture Union
207–209 Queensway, Bletchley, Milton Keynes, MK2 2EB
Email: info@scriptureunion.org.uk
Website: www.scriptureunion.org.uk

Scripture Union Australia
Locked Bag 2, Central Coast Business Centre, NSW 2252
Website: www.scriptureunion.org.au

Scripture Union USA
PO Box 987, Valley Forge, PA 19482
Website: www.scriptureunion.org

Scripture quotations are from the Contemporary English Version published by HarperCollins*Publishers* © 1991, 1992, 1995 American Bible Society.

British Library Cataloguing-in-Publication Data
A catalogue record of this book is available from the British Library.

Printed and bound by Nutech Print Services, India.

Cover design: Dodo Mammoth Reindeer Fox

Scripture Union is an international charity working with churches in more than 130 countries, providing resources to bring the good news of Jesus Christ to children, young people and families and to encourage them to develop spiritually through the Bible and prayer.

As well as our network of volunteers, staff and associates who run holidays, church-based events and school Christian groups, we produce a wide range of publications and support those who use our resources through training programmes.

Chapter 1:
Cooking for dummies

I learned a lot after Mum left. I learned that clothes don't wash themselves and houses don't clean themselves. And food doesn't magically appear when you need it.

I learned, by trial and error, how to cook. If Ben and I hadn't managed to do that, we would have starved, because Dad didn't get home from work until 6 or 7 o'clock. When Mum left, Ben was 13 and I was 9, and we didn't have a clue about cooking. We lived mostly on pizzas, sausages and fish fingers. Do you think that sounds good? It isn't. Not after the first month or so.

After a while we got a system going. Ben cooked on Mondays, Wednesdays and Fridays. I did Tuesdays and Thursdays, and Dad took over at the weekends. We started to experiment. We tried different things from TV programmes and recipe books.

It's amazing how quickly you can learn things when you really need to know them – not like in school. I am not a quick learner in school because I'm dyslexic, so I'm useless at reading and writing. Anyway, I don't care about school stuff. Maths and RE and history – what use will they ever be to you when you're hungry? But I can read a recipe book when I have to.

I did make a few mistakes. Well, how was I to know that *1 tbsp* wasn't the same as *1 tsp*? The chilli con carne was hotter than a volcano. We ate it, though.

After a few months of this, Ben said we should write a cookery book. I could think of the ideas and he would write them down. We could call it *Cooking for Dummies*, or maybe *Beans on toast in six easy lessons, as seen on TV*. It would be full of useful tips, such as:

1 *Don't panic if something goes wrong.*
2 *You can always cut off the burnt bits and serve up the rest.*
3 *If gravy goes lumpy, whisk it with an egg-beater.*
4 *Any food that falls on the floor is safe to eat if you pick it up in less than five seconds. (Possibly not soup, though.)*
5 *You don't have to follow every single word of a recipe.*
6 *If you haven't got something that's on the list, just forget it – nobody will notice.*
7 *Never eat chicken which is still pink in the middle. (It made us ill for three days.)*
8 *Always eat some of the food you've made, or people will be suspicious.*
9 *It is pointless trying to clean a really blackened pan – throw it away.*
10 *If you have a total disaster, there's always beans on toast.*

When I cooked something really excellent – which did happen sometimes – I felt great. I began to wonder if I could be a chef when I grew up. Maybe even a famous chef on TV, like that Jamie guy. He's dyslexic too, did you know?

And Dad would say, "Good work, Paul. We're doing really well, lads. Who needs women, eh?"

But we didn't manage so well with other things that Mum used to do, like housework. Dad got a cleaning lady to come in twice a week, but she was a real pain. She used to tidy things up so that we couldn't find them again. He told her not to put things away, just keep the place clean.

"How can I hoover when there's trainers and things all over the floor?" she asked.

"Just hoover round them, can't you?"

So the house was a bit of a mess. (But a fairly *clean* mess.) The laundry basket was always overflowing, and nothing got ironed until the moment it was needed. Dad got pretty good at ironing his work shirt while eating toast and drinking coffee.

And we were always late for everything. You would think Mum had been the only one who understood the use of clocks.

When she left, we didn't believe she had gone for ever. She had been saying things like, "I need my own space," and "I have to discover what I want out of life." Stupidly, we thought that when she had done that, she might come home to us.

But soon we found out the real reason she had gone. She'd fallen in love with a guy called Mike Fletcher. He was her best friend's husband. They went off together to live in Canada, "to make a fresh start," they said.

They didn't seem to care that they had broken up two families. All they cared about was themselves. I came to see that Mum didn't really love me. She didn't love any of us. Not enough to matter – not enough to make her want to stay with us.

At first she called us every week, but as time went on the calls got fewer and further between. And I never knew what to say on the phone. I couldn't tell her about the things that really mattered to me. If I'd got in trouble at school, or caught flu, or had a row with Ben, there was no point telling Mum about it. She was thousands of miles away. What could she do?

★ ★ ★

Mike Fletcher's family lived in Mallenford, the nearest town. His wife's name was Rushani. She had a daughter called Sophie, the same age as Ben – they were actually born on the same day in the same hospital, which was how Mum and Rushani got to know each other. There was also a boy, Danny, a few months younger than me, and a toddler called Will.

When we were younger, we sometimes went out for the day with the Fletchers. This was mainly because Mum and Rushani were friends. I didn't like Danny much, and Ben thought Sophie was too girly. She couldn't even kick a football straight.

We would go to the zoo, or wherever, and the two mums would talk non-stop about nothing much, like mums do. Dad and Mike Fletcher would argue about football. Dad hardly seemed to notice Rushani Fletcher in those days. I don't remember seeing him talk to her much.

But after Mum left, he started going round to call on her now and then. Maybe it was because they'd both been hurt by people that they loved. They had something to talk about now.

One day, Dad said casually to Ben and me, "How would you feel about us going on holiday with the Fletchers?"

"With the Fletchers? Why?" I said.

Ben said, "Are you going out with Rushani Fletcher, Dad?"

Dad looked slightly embarrassed. "You could say that. Although we don't actually go out much. We can't afford it."

"All right, are you seeing her?" I demanded.

"Well, she's not the Invisible Woman. Of course I see her when I go round there," Dad said.

"But are you… are you…?"

"Are we dating?" He made it sound like something in an old-fashioned movie. "Yes. I suppose we are."

Mum had gone off with Mike Fletcher. Now Dad was "dating" Rushani Fletcher. I couldn't get my head around it.

"That's weird," Ben said. "It's like that *Wife Swap* programme."

"What will Mum think about it?" I said.

"Strangely enough, I don't really care what your mother thinks," Dad said quite sharply.

Your mother. As if she was nothing to do with Dad any more. Well, that was true enough. But I didn't believe him when he said he didn't care.

"Anyway, the holiday. What do you think?" he asked us.

"Do we have to go?" I said. Ben said nothing at all.

So we all went to Norfolk for a week, staying in two separate caravans. It wasn't too bad. In fact it was better than I expected. We didn't have to mix too much with the Fletcher kids if we didn't want to. When we got tired of Danny arguing and Will pestering us to play with him, we had our own caravan to go to.

Dad and Rushani seemed very happy all through that week. Walking on the beach, they held hands like two kids. I hated to watch them.

To me, they just didn't look right together. Rushani, who was born in Sri Lanka, had big brown eyes and long dark hair. She was very pretty, small and slim. Dad was tall and broad, with fair hair (what was left of it).

They looked like they'd met through a computer-dating site where Dad had cheated by using a much younger photo of himself. Rushani still looked about 25, which was impossible, unless she'd got married at 11 years old. She was probably in her thirties, like Dad.

She was too good-looking for him. She would only let him down and hurt him, just like Mum did.

"Do you think they'll get married?" I asked Ben.

"I wouldn't be surprised," he said. "What's the matter? Don't you like the idea?"

"No!"

"Don't you think Dad deserves a bit of happiness?"

"Of course he does," I said. "But... oh, I don't know... if they get married, everything will change. I like things the way they are. I've got used to it."

Ben said, "That's not the real reason. You're still hoping Mum will come back one day, aren't you?"

I nodded.

"Face it, Paul, that's not going to happen. Not ever. She's gone."

Chapter 2:
It won't be for ever

Six months after the Norfolk holiday, Dad told us he had asked Rushani to marry him. And this time he didn't ask us what we thought of the idea. It was going to happen whether we liked it or not.

"Don't you think it's a bit too soon?" I tried to say to him.

"Soon? We've been going out for nearly a year. Anyway, it's not going to be tomorrow. We have to wait until the divorces are finalised. And it may take months to sort out the house."

"It's not *that* untidy, Dad," I said.

"I don't mean tidy it up. This house isn't big enough for seven people – same with Rushani's place. What we're planning is, we'll extend this house into the barn. I got planning permission to do that ages ago, but I never got around to it because…"

Because Mum left. He didn't have to say the words.

"Oh! Will we have to move out?"

"I hope not. I hope we can still live here while they do most of the work."

Ben got quite keen on the idea. "How big will the new part be?"

"Three extra bedrooms, so each of you can have your own room. Plus a good-sized kitchen and two bathrooms, and an attic room where you lot can hang out."

"Cool. We could have a pool table," said Ben.

I still wasn't keen on the idea. The Fletchers would be moving into our house and taking it over. It wouldn't be ours any more. Everything would change.

Dad saw my face, and sighed. "Look, Paul, give this marriage a chance, will you? Rushani is really nice. She's not going to turn into an evil stepmother, like in a fairy-tale."

"Dad, I'm not stupid," I said.

"What are you so worried about?"

"I'm afraid it will all go wrong. We won't get on with her kids. She'll want to keep the place all neat and tidy. We'll have to fit in with how they do things, and…"

Struggling for a way to explain myself, I saw some broken eggshells on the worktop. (I was in the middle of making an omelette for Dad's supper.)

"Look, Dad. Our family got broken up when Mum left, and so did theirs. But if we try to join the two broken pieces together, they won't fit. See?"

I picked up two pieces of shell from different eggs. There was no way of fitting them together to make one smooth egg-shape. They were just too different.

"I see what you're trying to say," said Dad. "But who says families are like eggshells? Maybe they're more like the inside bits of the egg. You can mix them together and cook something really nice."

"I don't *want* to be mixed up with the Fletchers. I like things the way they are."

"Well, I don't," Dad said. "I've had enough of being lonely. I'm tired of struggling along as a single dad. I've tried to do my best, but look at this place! Anybody can see that you boys need a mother."

I said, "Rushani isn't our mother. Never was. Never will be."

"I can smell something burning," Ben said.

I snatched the pan off the gas. Too late – the omelette was black underneath. Totally ruined.

"Looks like beans on toast again," Dad said wearily.

* * *

The work on the barn began.

Our house had a barn because it used to be a farmhouse. When the old farmer died, a neighbouring farmer bought the land and sold off the house. It wasn't a huge house – three bedrooms, with a bathroom downstairs. Dad and Mum bought it, planning to extend it, but that had never happened. The barn, an empty space bigger than the house, became a garage and a place to dump things.

It was quite interesting seeing the work begin... like one of those TV makeover programmes for houses. The difference is, the TV only shows you the highlights, and it seems to be done super-quick. In reality the work went on for months, and still the inside of the building looked more like a climbing-frame than a house.

Then Dad had an argument with the builder, who wanted some money up front. Dad couldn't pay him until Rushani sold her house, which was taking ages. The builder said he couldn't do any more work without getting paid. So work came to a complete stop.

I didn't mind. I thought it would mean the wedding would be delayed. But then somebody saw the Fletchers' house and liked it. The trouble was, he was keen to move in straight away.

"We'll get married on the day we planned," Dad told us, "even though the house won't be finished. We can live with a few weeks of chaos, can't we?"

"You have got to be kidding," said Ben. "Seven people in this house?"

"Can't they rent somewhere until this place is ready?" I asked.

"We can't afford that," said Dad. "Money's quite tight already without throwing it away on rent."

So they got married just before my 12th birthday. Some birthday present!

It was supposed to be a small, quiet wedding, but somehow the plans got bigger as time went on. Dad hired the village hall, and some of Rushani's friends organised a buffet meal. There must have been over 60 guests there. I hardly knew any of them.

It felt strange, seeing Dad and Rushani standing side by side. I still didn't think they belonged together. And Sophie, Danny and Will didn't look like they belonged with Ben and me. It was obvious we were from two different families, one lot slim and dark-haired, the others big-boned and fair. Nothing, not even cosmetic surgery and hair dye, would ever make us look like brothers and sisters.

We were all dressed up. I felt like an idiot, wearing a suit that we'd bought in the Oxfam shop. "The rate you're growing, it's daft to buy you a new suit that you'll only wear once or twice," Dad had said.

"Once or twice? When's your next wedding going to be, then, Dad?"

"Never. This one's going to last."

"You hope," I said.

Before the meal, we had to pose for photos. "And now let's have one of the whole family," the photographer shouted.

In the photo, Dad and Rushani were wearing Lottery-winner smiles. Sophie was pouting and posing like a model. Ben and I stood shoulder to shoulder, stiff and unsmiling. Danny was scowling, and 4-year-old Will looked as if he was about to cry.

"Oh! Isn't that lovely?" I heard an old lady say. "Two families becoming one!"

"She's either short-sighted or senile," Ben whispered to me.

When Dad and Rushani came back from their honeymoon (two nights in Scarborough), Rushani's family moved in. It was really impossible to fit them all in, but somehow we did it.

Ben had to sleep on an air bed in the tiny room we called the office. Sophie, as the only girl, got a proper bedroom – Ben's old room. Danny, Will and I had to share the biggest bedroom, which used to be Dad's. Dad and Rushani moved into my room.

"And when the music stops," said Dad, "the person without a bed is out."

Nobody laughed.

"It will not be for ever," said Rushani. "The builders are starting work again next week. Soon everyone will have a room of their own."

"I'm not sure I can survive till then," muttered Danny, "without murdering Will."

I felt I wanted to murder the whole lot of them. I was used to having my own space where I could do what I liked – use my PlayStation, play my electronic drums, and leave my clothes on the floor. Now I was crammed into one corner of a room, with all my things in boxes, as if I was the one who'd had to move house.

Danny and I were totally different. You could tell that just by looking at our belongings. He had about six boxes of books, a saxophone, an astronomical telescope, and every Dr Who DVD in the entire known universe.

"I thought you were only supposed to bring essential things," I said to him. (Most of the Fletchers' furniture had been put in storage until the house was ready.)

"What do you mean? These are essential things," he said. "My telescope should work really well out here in the country. There was too much light pollution in town."

His big sister was just the opposite. She hated living outside of town. "This is so boring," she was moaning after the first day or two. "How am I going to meet up with my friends? I can't even phone them, the signal's so bad out here."

Amazingly, Dad and Rushani were still looking very happy. How long was that going to last?

And then something happened to take my mind off all this.

I saw a UFO.

Chapter 3:
The thing

It happened in the middle of the night. A strange noise woke me – after a minute I realised that it was Danny snoring. He could snore for England. That was another downside of sharing a bedroom.

Now that I was awake, I found I needed the loo. This meant going all the way downstairs, and by the time I came back I was as wide awake as a 5-year-old on Christmas Eve.

I got bored lying in bed, staring at nothing. After a while I got up again. Danny had said there was supposed to be a meteor storm that night. He had wanted to stay up and watch it, but when Rushani found out that it would be at its height at around 2am, she wouldn't let him.

"You have to go to school tomorrow. You would be asleep at your desk, all because of a few shooting stars! No, Danny."

Sometimes Rushani sounded very like a teacher. In fact, she used to be a teacher before she had kids, and she was hoping to go back to it one day, when Will started school. Meanwhile she was using her own kids to keep her hand in. She was very strict about homework and stuff.

Fortunately she hadn't started on that with Ben and me... not yet anyway.

Danny looked annoyed, but he didn't argue. I wondered if he was planning to wake up anyway, after everyone had gone to bed, and I offered to lend him my alarm clock.

"Thanks," he said, looking surprised. "But don't worry. It's pretty cloudy tonight. Probably there won't be anything to see."

"What is a... what's name... meteor storm, anyway?"

He went off into a long explanation about comets and asteroids. I had already sussed that Danny was quite clever. We were both in Year 7 at school, but not the same class, which was lucky – he would only show me up.

Now he was snoring peacefully and I was awake. My clock said 3:10. I decided to look for the meteor storm. Maybe, if there was anything worth seeing, I would wake him up.

In daylight there was a good view from the front window because our house was halfway up a hill. We looked out over fields and woods, with hardly any houses in sight. At night it was very dark. The only light was a pale orange glow low down on the horizon, coming from the town, four miles away.

That night, half the sky was cloudy. In the other half, the stars shone very bright. But nothing was moving – maybe Danny had got the date wrong?

Then I saw a shooting star... a tiny point of light which seemed to appear from nowhere. Moving so fast that I would have missed it if I'd blinked, it shot across the sky and disappeared beyond the distant hills.

Half a minute later I saw another one – no, two. Then nothing for a while. This wasn't exactly a storm, more of a drizzle. I wondered why Danny had been so keen to see it.

I was finally starting to feel a bit sleepy. Just as I was about to go back to bed, I noticed another light. This one was low down in the sky, moving much more slowly than the shooting stars. At first I thought it was a plane. But the light was steady. It didn't blink on and off like aeroplane lights.

As it came closer, I saw there were actually three lights in a triangle shape. They moved erratically – not like a plane, more like a helicopter piloted by a complete beginner. They went sideways, came to a stop, then slid towards me again.

If they belonged to a helicopter, I ought to be able to hear it by now. I slid the window open and felt the cool night air drifting in. But no sound came with it. The night was totally silent.

Now I could see a dark shape, a sort of black hole in the starlit sky. An oval kind of shape, like a frisbee coming towards me in slow motion. It wasn't like any plane, helicopter or hang-glider that I had ever seen. It was more like a... flying saucer?

"Danny. Danny! Come and see this!"

He woke up slowly and groggily. "What's the matter?"

"I think it's a UFO! Quick. Where's your telescope?"

Still half asleep, Danny staggered across the room, tripping over Will on his mattress-bed. He was just in time to see the dark shape with its three lights. It slid out of view above the window – right over the house.

We ran to the small window at the back. Out here we could see nothing except trees and stars. Had I imagined the whole thing? Or was the strange shape sitting motionless above our roof, like a hovering bird of prey?

A curved edge of darkness slid forwards, blanking out the stars. We saw the lights again. We saw the size of the thing – enormous. To me, it looked wider than the wingspan of a jumbo jet. Wider than the entire house.

"What is it?" I whispered.

"How should I know?" He was whispering too, as if the thing might hear us.

For a few seconds more we watched it. Still completely silent, it slipped away to the north, disappearing over the trees behind the house.

I took a long breath. I realised that I must have stopped breathing for a minute.

"Was it really a UFO?" I said. "I never believed in that sort of stuff. You know… aliens from outer space."

He said, "It may not be full of aliens. But it was a flying object we can't identify. That's what UFO means. Unidentified Flying Object."

He often talked like that – like a professor in a movie, brilliant but a bit mad.

"Do you think it was coming in to land?" I asked. "It was flying pretty low."

"You can't say that. We don't actually know how low it was because we don't know its size. It could be a mile above us and 5 miles wide."

"But if it was that high, we wouldn't have seen the lights."

"We don't know what alien technology can do."

"So you do think it's full of aliens!"

Suddenly the bedroom light went on, making me blink. Rushani was standing in the doorway, with Will clutching her dressing-gown.

"What are you doing?" she said crossly. "Danny, I told you not to stay up to watch stars! And now you have awakened Will, and frightened him. And you will be asleep in school tomorrow."

"I *didn't* stay up," said Danny. "Paul woke me, and we saw—"

"No, you woke me first with your snoring," I said.

"Mum, we saw a UFO! I'm not making this up. It went right over the house!"

"I think you have been dreaming," said Rushani.

"I saw it too," I said. "We can't both have had the same dream."

"I'm scared," Will whimpered. "I don't want to live here any more. I want to go home."

"Be quiet, all of you, and get back into your beds," Rushani said.

Will clung to her legs. "I'm frightened, Mum!"

"Now see what you have done!" She was very angry. "All right, Will, bring your sleeping bag. You can sleep in our room tonight. Danny, Paul, get into bed NOW!"

She snapped the light off.

Lying in bed, I whispered to Danny, "We did see it, though."

"Yes. It was real. It definitely was not a dream."

"I wonder if it landed somewhere."

"We'll go and have a look in the morning," said Danny.

He sounded excited – not at all worried. Maybe he thought it would be like on Dr Who. Aliens invade… cities are attacked, people get killed… then the Doctor saves the world for the 500th time.

There is no Dr Who, I wanted to tell him. If there really are aliens invading earth, who will save us?

Chapter 4:
Mystery object

In the morning there was no time to go looking for the UFO. We had all overslept. Rushani, who was usually the first to get up, had slept right through the alarm. It was chaos as we took turns to use the only bathroom, and shovelled down some breakfast, and ran for the school bus.

On the bus, I tried to tell Ben what we had seen. He didn't really believe us. Like Rushani, he thought we must have been dreaming.

"Or else you saw a test flight of a new military plane, or something," he said.

"Ben, I know what a plane looks like."

"You don't know what the next generation of planes will look like, though," he said. "There's an air base at Murrayhill. They might be doing test flights over Rawton Moor at night."

Rawton Moor lay over the hill at the back of our house. It was a wide area of marshy moorland, empty apart from sheep... a perfect place for secret test flights. And the Thing had certainly been heading in that direction.

Danny turned round from the seat in front. "So, you think they've discovered a totally new way of flying? Hovering like a helicopter, but silently?"

"It's possible."

"But unlikely," I said.

Ben said, "Not as unlikely as little grey men from outer space."

"Is Rawton Moor private land, or can anybody go there?" asked Danny.

"Anybody can. But not many people bother. There's nothing there except hills and marshes and sheep."

"We ought to go and have a look after school," Danny said. "You know you said the Thing might be looking for a place to land? If it did land, we might find signs."

"What kind of signs?" I asked him.

"I don't know – scorch marks on the grass, perhaps. Or crop circles."

Ben snorted. "Crop circles! They're just a hoax. And anyway there aren't any crops on the moor."

Danny said, "I still think it's worth a look. We might even find the crashed remains of the UFO – like at Roswell."

I didn't know what he meant by that. He explained to me, "Some people think a UFO crash-landed in a desert in America, 50 years ago. But the government hushed it all up."

"And some people think that's a load of cods," said Ben.

All the same, he was getting interested – I could tell. Coming back home on the bus after school, the three of us decided to explore the moor, or as much of it as we could before it got dark. We got changed and put on boots, except for Danny, who didn't have any.

Rushani looked pleased when she saw Danny going with us... but not quite so pleased when he told her why. (She still didn't believe we had actually seen anything the night before.)

"I want to go too," said Will.

We looked at each other. "He'll only slow us down," said Ben.

When his mum told him he couldn't go, Will launched into a huge tantrum, kicking and shouting. We left hurriedly, leaving his mum to cope with him.

"Your brother's a pain," I said to Danny.

"Yeah. He's always been like that, but he got worse after our dad left."

This was the first time I'd ever heard Danny mention his dad. But then I didn't talk about Mum much, either. It was like Mum and Mike had vanished off the face of the earth. (Possibly abducted by aliens.)

We went up through the wood behind the house. From the top of the hill, we could see the moor spread out in front of us. There were low hills, boggy valleys, and a few twisted trees. It was October, and the days were getting shorter. The sun cast long shadows across the moor.

"I always thought this place was kind of spooky," I said.

"It's pretty empty," said Danny. "Just the sort of place they would like."

Ben said, "They? You mean aliens… little grey men?"

"I mean anyone who doesn't want to be seen."

Ben had brought Dad's ancient binoculars. He scanned the moor carefully. Suddenly he drew in his breath.

"What is it? What can you see?" Danny demanded.

"I can see a little grey…"

"What?"

"Wait a minute… yes! It is! It's a little grey sheep!"

I thought this was funny, but Danny didn't. He tried to grab the binoculars. Ben refused to let him have them, and Danny looked moody. If he got into one of his silent moods, it might last all evening.

"Come on," I said, "we're wasting time. We don't have long before dark."

We set out across the moor, keeping to the hills whenever we could because the ground was drier. There was nothing much to see. A bird of prey hovered on the breeze. A few sheep kept an eye on us, moving away when we got too close.

The moor looked just the way it always did. There was no sign of the mysterious Thing which might have passed over it a few hours before. And the sun was getting quite low now.

"Better not go too far," I said uneasily.

"Not scared, are you?" asked Ben.

"No, hungry. And Rushani doesn't like it if people are late for meals."

We swung round in a wide curve which would take us back over some different ground. This was a mistake. We had to cross a wide area of marsh, where the thick mud almost dragged the boots off our feet. Danny's trainers looked as if they would never be white again.

At last we got clear of the bog. We followed the line of a broken fence, where the wind made a low moaning in the wires. Not far to go now. I felt I would be glad to get off the moor... This had been a complete waste of time.

All at once, Danny stopped.

"What's that?" he said.

He was pointing at something on the ground. A scattering of small stones, I thought at first. But the stones of the moor were mostly grey – these things were white and sort of see-through, like jelly. They looked a little bit like frogspawn, without the dark centre where the tadpole develops.

I hadn't a clue what they were. Neither did Ben.

"You ought to know," Danny said. "You live in the country."

"So do you, now," I reminded him. "It doesn't mean you've suddenly turned into David Attenborough."

"I would have said they were frogspawn, except that it's the wrong time of year," said Ben.

We looked around. I didn't remember noticing any frogs in the marshy areas we had crossed.

"What happens to frogs in the winter?" asked Danny. "Do they die off?"

"No idea. Maybe they hibernate, or something," said Ben.

Danny bent down to have a closer look at the white blobs of jelly. He put out his hand towards one.

"Don't touch it!" I said.

"Why not?"

"It looks disgusting. All slimy, like snot."

"Snot?" said Danny. "What kind of animal produces snot like that?

Ben laughed. "Maybe those aliens of yours had a cold."

Danny stared at him. I could see an idea coming into his head, almost like a cartoon light bulb coming on.

"Yes! Of course!" he said. "It can't be a coincidence. Last night we saw a UFO. Today we find this stuff."

Ben laughed again. "I was joking, you idiot. You don't really think this is the snot of aliens?"

"No," said Danny. "I think it's the eggs of aliens. We ought to destroy them before it's too late."

He wasn't joking. He was perfectly serious.

"But then it probably is too late," he said. "This won't be the only place where they've planted their eggs. They could be everywhere – all over the world. We'll never find them all."

Chapter 5:
School report

Ben said, "That's just stupid. The eggs of aliens!"

"It's not stupid," Danny said angrily. "If they're nothing to do with the UFO, why did we find them the very day after we saw it?"

"Because we came out here, that's why," said Ben. "They could have been here for weeks. We just happened to find them today because we came looking for the UFO. They're probably not connected at all."

"You don't know anything about it, so shut up," said Danny angrily.

"Don't tell me to shut up, kid."

Oh-oh. This was turning into a full-scale row.

I said, "Can't we discuss this later? It'll be dark soon."

The sun had completely gone. There was still a bit of light in the sky, but the first stars were coming out. The forest along the edge of the moor looked dark and threatening.

Danny said, "We should tell somebody about this."

"Like who? Go on, call the police," Ben said mockingly. "Call 999! I've found some frogspawn!"

"You said yourself, it's the wrong time of year for frogspawn. Why aren't you taking this seriously?"

"Because you talk such total rubbish!"

They faced each other like two boxers. Danny, small and slim-built like his mum, would be no match for Ben if it came to a fight. I tried to calm things down.

"Maybe we could put this on the Internet," I said. "See if anyone else has found that jelly stuff. Find out more about it."

Both of them stared at me, as if they hated me for interfering. Then Ben said, "I suppose I could take some photos with my phone."

"Good idea," said Danny.

Because of the fading light, the pictures weren't wonderful. But we didn't have time to mess about. We hurried down through the trees towards home.

Rushani was looking out anxiously. "Oh, there you are," she said, relieved. "I was starting to think you must be lost, and I couldn't get through on your mobile."

"I was hoping the aliens had got you," said Sophie. "They must have decided you weren't worth it."

"Everybody thinks this is just a joke," Danny muttered. "But they're so wrong. They'll find out soon enough."

We had supper and then, after heaving Ben's air bed out of the office, we managed to get to our computer. (Danny's family owned a computer too, but it was still in a box because there was nowhere to put it.)

Ben did a search on *jelly*, which found thousands of food-related results... orange jelly, jelly beans, jelly roll, gelatine, and could you really nail jelly to a wall? (No, was the answer.) *Frogspawn* and *alien eggs* weren't too helpful either. *Rawton Moor UFO* found no results at all.

"Let's see if the photos can help," he said.

He uploaded the photos from his phone, and posted them on several different websites.

"What do we do next?" asked Danny.

"We wait for a day or two and see if anybody replies," said Ben. "Now, can you all get out of my room?"

★ ★ ★

Danny and I had both started at Mallenford High School a few weeks before. Danny seemed quite happy there, but I didn't like it. It was the total opposite of the village school I used to go to, where there were only two teachers and 40 kids all together. The high school had 150 pupils in each year, and dozens of teachers.

At the village school, my teacher knew I was dyslexic and made allowances for it. She gave me extra time to read and write things, and didn't mind too much if I made spelling mistakes. But the teachers at senior school were always rushing us along. Most of them didn't have time to explain things that I found hard to read. And everything I wrote came back covered in corrections.

After a while I stopped wanting to write anything at all. I would come to a word that I wasn't sure how to spell, stop writing and just sit there.

There was another boy in my class with the same problem – Tom Weston. We both got told off a lot. One day we got a lunchtime detention together, and spent the time moaning about school.

"I hate this place," I said. "I wish I was still at junior school."

"I hate all schools. I can't wait to leave. Five years to go… it's like a prison sentence."

"Yeah. And we haven't even committed a crime."

"Is your dad going to the parents' evening?" Tom asked me.

"What parents' evening?"

"The one in that letter old Fuzzface gave us today." He tried to copy our form teacher's voice. "Don't you ever listen, Paul? Clean your ears out!"

"My dad doesn't usually bother with things like that," I said. "He doesn't get home from work in time."

"Lucky you," said Tom. "If my dad knows I'm getting in trouble at school, he'll stop my pocket money. I think I'll just forget to take the letter home." He took it out of his pocket, screwed it up and lobbed it in the bin.

I did the same. But that was pointless, because Danny had a letter too, and he gave it to his mum like a good little boy. So Dad found out about the meeting, and Rushani made sure he went to it. We all went – Dad, Rushani, Danny and me – like four cards from a carelessly shuffled *Happy Families* game.

I had a bad feeling about this. The feeling got worse as we scurried around the school, trying to spend five minutes with each of my teachers and Danny's too. I didn't go into the classrooms when it was Danny's turn, but I could usually see through the glass of the doors.

Each time, the teacher was smiling. Danny was *such* a good pupil… not like me.

None of my teachers had a good word to say about me. I was too slow. I was careless. My spelling and handwriting were poor. I didn't listen, and I distracted other pupils. (Just because Tom and I used to talk to each other when we got bored.)

Sitting outside the science lab while Danny was inside, I kicked my legs and felt resentful. How come "reports" always meant teachers reporting on pupils? We ought to be allowed to assess the teachers and their subjects. That was only fair.

School Report on Mallenford High School

Games:	7/10 (unless it's cross-country, 1/10).
Art:	3/10
Drama:	5/10 (because Miss Ross is a good laugh)
Technology:	2/10
Maths:	$2/10 = 1/5 = 20\ \%$
French:	nul points
Spanish:	nada
Science:	$H2010$
History:	1-10 A.D.
Geography:	3:10 (I quite like maps and stuff)
English:	zero, nothing, nought, nil, zilch
RE:	zzzzzzzzzz…ero
In general:	A poor performance. Could do better.

The classroom door opened and Danny came out, looking pleased with himself. I wanted to kick him.

"Your turn," he said cheerfully. Although we were in different classes, we happened to have the same science teacher, Mr Martin.

I sat down next to Dad and Rushani. Mr Martin's face turned grim and serious. I stopped listening pretty soon, because it was all the same kind of stuff. *Hasn't made a very good start… could do much better if he was prepared to put in some effort…*

Then Rushani spoke for the first time. Up to now she had been letting my dad do the talking.

She said, "Excuse me. Do you take any account of the fact that Paul is dyslexic?"

"Well, yes. But dyslexia is no excuse for not trying. Paul has not been doing his science homework, and in class he often sits there without writing anything at all. He can also be quite disruptive."

"Disruptive?"

"By being noisy. Talking too much. He seems to think he is a comedian, your son. But the place for that is outside the classroom."

Mr Martin looked at me with dislike. Not for the first time, I noticed his weird eyes. They seemed to look in slightly different directions. Probably quite useful for a teacher – he could keep an eye on two people at once – but it made him look odd. Abnormal.

"And two days ago," he went on, "during an experiment, I found Paul and another boy playing around with a Bunsen burner. Highly dangerous! If they do it again they will be banned from the laboratory."

He had a strange voice, too. It sounded as if he had a bad cold all the time, and he spoke with an accent that I couldn't recognise. He was a small man with grey-white hair and a greyish, unhealthy-looking face.

A small grey man... maybe he was an alien in disguise! Maybe his name should be Martian, not Martin! Must see what Tom thought of that idea.

He was still rabbiting on. "This kind of behaviour, right at the start of his senior school career, is a very bad sign. We do not want Paul to end up being excluded from school, do we? Or to leave at the age of 16 with no qualifications?"

Go on then, exclude me, I felt like saying. I don't care. It would be like getting let out of prison early... let out for bad behaviour instead of good.

"You can help your son improve. For one thing, you must make sure he does his homework. Check up on him. Don't just sign his homework diary automatically."

"I've never seen his homework diary," said Dad.

"But you appear to have signed it."

Big trouble! I had been writing Dad's signature (dead easy, it was just a scribble) to say that I had done my homework every night. I should have known I wouldn't get away with it for ever.

* * *

Later, when Dad got me on my own, he asked why I hadn't told him I was finding things hard at school.

There were so many answers to that, I didn't know where to start. Because he might get mad at me... because he had enough on his plate already... because Danny never had problems...

I said nothing. He sighed.

"Paul, I know this is a stressful time. You've had to cope with a lot of changes recently. New school, new family, alterations to the house, all at the same time. No wonder you're finding life hard. But we will get through this. We will – I promise."

How could he promise that? He hadn't even been able to stop Mum from leaving.

When I was little, I thought Dad was so clever, he could fix anything. But now I knew that he couldn't. There are things that nobody can fix – broken families, stressed-out people, fractured lives.

"If you have problems, I want you to come and tell me," Dad said. "Don't keep quiet about it. Talk to me. Will you do that?"

"Yes, all right."

But even as I said it, I knew it was a lie.

Chapter 6:

A hard slog

From then on, Rushani started acting like a teacher with me, as well as with her own kids. As soon as I got home from school, she made me sit down and do my homework. I hated that. If anyone was going to do this, it should have been Dad, not her. But Dad was having a busy time at work, never getting home 'til late.

In one way it was good. Rushani didn't mind helping me, so I didn't get stuck on words I couldn't spell. But she made me do reading practice like a 6-year-old.

"It's the only way you are going to get better at reading," she said. "And reading is so important, Paul. Reading is the key to everything."

She tried lots of things that were supposed to help me read better. A coloured plastic screen over the words... reading aloud with me... a stack of flash cards with words on them... But I didn't feel as if any of it was helping much.

The only thing it did was annoy Will, who didn't like his mum giving me so much of her attention. He would climb up on her knee when we were doing reading practice, and sit there sucking his thumb like a baby, although he was 4 years old.

After a few days, Will could read the flash cards better than I could. That was it. I refused to use them again.

But Rushani still made me do reading practice. When I complained to Dad, he sighed and said, "You should be grateful, Paul."

"Grateful!"

"Yes. It would be easy for Rushani not to bother. To leave me to take care of you and Ben."

"I wish she would do that," I muttered.

"But I just don't have the time to do what she's doing," said Dad. "It will be worth it in the end, if it helps your reading. A lot of things seem like a hard slog at the time, but they're worth it in the end."

"Oh yeah? Like marriage, you mean?"

"I was going to say, like waiting for the barn to be finished. It will be worth it in the end, and we'll forget how tough things were while we were waiting for it."

Things were definitely tough. With the seven of us all cooped up in a few small rooms, it felt like an explosion waiting to detonate. We had two TV sets, but nobody ever agreed about what to watch. Everyone would be desperate to use the computer at the same time, or the phone, or the bathroom.

And the noise could get pretty bad. The sound of power drills from the barn... Will and Danny fighting... Danny's saxophone practice... Ben and Sophie arguing... the two TVs competing with each other...

I longed to play my drums just to block it all out (using headphones, of course – I'm not totally selfish). But there was no room anywhere to set up the drum kit.

The barn was making progress. It had a new roof, with big skylight windows. Some of the floors were in place, and part of a staircase. You could start to picture what it would look like when it was finished – before Christmas, we were all hoping. "Don't count on it," Dad kept saying.

Rushani said, "I don't mind if the kitchen is not ready before Christmas. But it would be so nice if some of the bedrooms were finished."

"And the bathrooms," said Sophie longingly. None of us had had a bath in weeks. Dad had confiscated the bath plug so that we could only use the shower, which was quicker and used less water.

"And the attic room," said Danny. "I'm going to set up my telescope there."

"It better not get in the way of my drums," I said.

"Or my pool table," Ben put in.

"What about my train set?" said Will.

Danny said, "You won't be allowed in the attic, kid. It's going to be a chill-out place for us older ones."

"*Us older ones?*" Ben said scornfully. "You're the second-youngest, Danny. Maybe we won't let you in."

Danny said, "It's not up to you to decide. It's our money that's paying for all this, remember? Our money. From the sale of our house."

"I wish we never sold our house," said Will. "I wish we were still living there."

I think most of us were wishing the same thing.

★ ★ ★

A couple of weeks had gone by since we saw the UFO. Danny and I had woken up in the night a few times, and looked out of the window. But we hadn't seen it again.

There had been quite a bit of interest in the photos of the jelly-like stuff. People had posted replies on the Internet, with photos of similar stuff that they had found. It was usually seen in country places – the Scottish Highlands, the Welsh borders, or high on the Pennines. Nobody was 100 per cent sure what it was.

Possible explanations for the jelly:
– slime from mating slugs
– frogspawn that had never been fertilised
– pond scum caught up by a whirlwind
– remnants from a meteor shower
– absorbent stuff from inside a disposable nappy
– otter jelly
– elves with the flu
– nostoc, a freshwater bacteria which can form colonies on open ground (people eat it in China apparently).

"Yuk," said Danny. "I wouldn't eat that stuff."

We didn't think any of the explanations were correct. We hadn't seen any otters on the moor (or elves, for that matter). We hadn't noticed slugs mating in huge numbers. It wasn't spawning time for frogs. There hadn't been a whirlwind anywhere nearby. As for meteors, Danny said they got so hot as they approached the earth that anything jelly-like would be burnt away.

"Disposable nappy – that's just stupid. Why would anyone leave the insides of a nappy away out on the moor?" asked Danny.

"Maybe it got dumped from an aeroplane," I said.

"You can't throw things out of a plane just like that! It's pressurised. The windows and doors are sealed up."

"So, what does that leave us with?"

"Not a lot. Except for the thing I've been saying all along… alien eggs."

I tried to picture the blobs of jelly. They didn't seem much like eggs to me.

"I wonder if they're still there," I said. "We could go and have a look."

"They might have already hatched out into something," said Danny.

"What kind of something?"

"How would I know? Aliens could be anything. Monsters or humanoids, or giant snakes, or tiny little things the size of ants."

I thought I could cope with ants. Monsters and giant snakes I wasn't so sure about. But I didn't really believe in any of this. I thought Danny was crazy, taking it so seriously.

Danny said, "I'll ask Mum for a jam-jar to take with us. If the stuff is still there, I'll bring some back."

"What? You're going to try and grow aliens in a jar, like tadpoles?"

"No, I'm going to take the stuff to school and show it to Mr Martin. He'll know what it is – he's a science teacher. Or at least he'll know how to do tests on it and find out what it's made of."

"Oh yeah, Mr Martian, the alien teacher. He'll know what it is, all right. But if he's part of the alien invasion force, he won't tell you, will he? He'll vaporise you with his alpha-particle phaser gun."

"Shut up," said Danny. Like a lot of clever people, he didn't have much sense of humour.

We decided to go out jelly-hunting the next morning. It was the first day of half-term, so we would have plenty of time to explore the moor. I wanted to ask Ben to come too, but Danny wouldn't let me. He said that if Ben came along, he would stay at home.

When Rushani realised that Ben wasn't with us, she looked rather anxious. But she didn't stop us going.

"Don't get lost." she said. "Be back before dark."

"Rushani, it's only the moor, not Mount Everest," I said. "We'll be back in a couple of hours. No problem."

"You worry too much, Mum," said Danny.

Both of us were wrong.

Chapter 7:

Circles

"Huh! Mum's worried about us getting lost, when there are a lot worse things that might happen to us," Danny said when we were outside.

"Like what? Getting your trainers muddy again?" I said.

"Getting abducted by aliens."

"Yeah. In your dreams."

We set off up the hill. The sky was dark with low-lying cloud. This worried me a bit, because if it got misty out on the moor, we really might get lost. There were not many landmarks out there to guide us.

"We'll be all right if we stay near that fence," Danny said confidently. "The eggs were quite close to the fence – remember?"

"Good thinking, Batman."

We left the shelter of the woods and followed the line of the old fence. But we walked for quite a distance without seeing the jelly blobs.

"I'm sure we should have seen them by now," I said.

"Yeah, you're right. They've disappeared."

"Maybe the sheep ate them."

Danny said, "If those were eggs, and they hatched, the next stage of development could be quite different. You know, like caterpillars or birds or snakes – totally different from the eggs that they hatch out from."

I looked around. "Well, unless they hatched out into sheep or clumps of grass, I can't see anything they could have turned into."

"Perhaps the next stage is invisible," said Danny. "Or perhaps it lives in the marsh – those things could be amphibious, like frogs. Or if a sheep did swallow an egg, the next stage might be a parasite, growing inside the sheep's stomach."

"Danny, you have quite an imagination. You ought to write science fiction."

"That's what I'd like to do," he said, quite seriously.

"Really?"

He hesitated. "Don't tell anyone… I've already started writing a book. It's on our computer, so I can't write any more at the moment."

"What's it about?"

He started telling me about an expedition to a distant galaxy inhabited by mind-reading purple aliens. It sounded a bit like an old repeat of Star Trek, but I didn't say so.

By now the fence had come to an end. In front of us was the wide stretch of marsh that I remembered from our last visit. "I'm not going through that boggy bit again," I said.

We looked around. Was I imagining it, or did the clouds seem lower? They made everything look grey… the sky, the hills, the marsh. The sheep, of course, were already grey. It was all rather depressing.

Danny said, "It's pretty boring to go back the same way. We could go along the higher ground, towards that wall, see?" He was pointing to a stone wall running across a nearby hill. "We'd be covering some new territory then, and we might find some more eggs."

"OK."

We followed the curve of a low hill. A dead tree stood in our path, and as we walked round it, Danny said, "There! Look!"

Scattered across the grass were more of the whitish blobs. They looked just the same as last time, small and round and jelly-like, almost see-through. I counted at least 30 of them.

Danny had put a few items in my backpack, including a camera. He took it out. To give an idea of how big the jelly blobs were, he laid a key alongside them. Then he photographed them from several different angles.

We had also brought a jam-jar and a plastic spoon. Danny scooped several of the things up, being careful not to touch them. I thought that was a wise move, whatever they turned out to be. Bacteria, slug slime, nappy contents or alien parasites… all of them were things you wouldn't want to touch.

He screwed the top on the jar and put it away. As we stood up, we got a shock. The cloud had come down all around us – a pale grey mist, chilly as the touch of a ghost. We couldn't see more than a few yards in any direction.

We decided it would be safer to go back the way we had come. But which direction was that? I pointed one way. Danny pointed in a completely different direction. There was nothing to see except the dead tree, the mist, and the grassy hilltop.

"Maybe we should wait here for a while until the mist lifts," I said.

We waited for five minutes, which felt more like an hour. The mist seemed to be getting thicker, and the air growing colder.

Danny said, "We can't sit here all day. That fog might last until night-time."

"If we walk in a straight line," I said, "we should find the fence or the wall."

But what we found was the edge of the marsh. That was the wrong direction – if we crossed it, we would be going further out onto the moor. So we swung to the right, looking for the old fence. We seemed to walk a long way, but we didn't see it.

Then we came to another marshy area, or maybe the same one – there was no way of knowing.

"This is stupid," Danny said. "I mean, it's not like we're in the middle of the Sahara Desert. How big is this moor?"

"I think it's about five miles across."

"So, whichever direction we go in, we should reach the edge of it eventually."

"Yes, if we could be sure we're walking in a straight line."

That was the trouble. We couldn't see more than a few yards ahead. It was impossible to know if we were walking straight or going in a circle.

"Which way now?" said Danny.

"How should I know?"

"We're lost, aren't we? I'm going to phone my mum."

I said, "How can she help? If she comes looking for us, she'll get lost too."

"I just want to talk to her. Tell her what's happening," said Danny. But he couldn't get a signal on his phone.

"Try your phone," he said.

"What phone? I haven't got one, remember?" I had lost mine a couple of weeks before, or maybe it had been nicked at school. As it was the third one I'd lost, Dad had refused to pay for another one.

I was starting to feel quite scared. I told myself not to be stupid – what could hurt you on the moor? There were no dangerous animals – nothing life-threatening. (Except perhaps the cold. If we did have to spend the night out here, we might get hypothermia and freeze to death.)

What if Danny was right about the aliens, though? What if they came back?

"Come on," I said. "Keep walking."

Something loomed through the mist. It was a dead tree… the same one as before? Surely not… But it looked exactly like the other one, and it had the same blobs of jelly around it.

"We're back where we started," I said in despair. "What do we do now?"

Chapter 8:

The trip

Danny said, "If only the mist would clear. Then we could aim for something and keep walking towards it. Or if we had a compass..."

"A compass! Wait a minute! There's just a chance – let me look."

I started digging everything out of the backpack. It wasn't actually mine – it was Ben's old one, which I'd borrowed without asking. Long ago, when he was in the Scouts, he used to take it on camps and midnight hikes.

In one of the pockets, along with a broken torch and a mouldy-looking Mars bar, I found it... a small compass, which must have been in there for years.

"I don't believe it," said Danny. "You had that with you all the time?"

"We don't know if it works or not – don't get too excited."

I held it flat, and the needle swung like something alive, and settled, quivering. The red end pointed north, the black end south. I knew that the moor lay to the north of our house. We just had to keep walking southwards and we would reach the edge of it.

"OK," I said. "Let's go home."

Ten minutes of walking, following the compass, and we reached the edge of the moor. We went down through the woods, with the mist clearing all the time.

By the time we got down to the fields, we were below the cloud level. We could easily see our house, a couple of fields away.

"Don't tell Mum we got lost," said Danny, "or she won't let us go out on the moors again."

"Are you mad? I'm not planning on going back there… not unless it's a bright, sunny day without a cloud in the sky."

Anyway, we had got what we came for – the jelly blobs. I asked Danny what he planned to do with them.

"Take them to school and show them to Mr Martin," he said.

"Yeah, but before that. Where will you put them while we're away?"

Danny and I were going to the Lake District for part of half-term. It was a trip organised by the youth group from the church that Rushani belonged to. Danny had persuaded me to go along with him. I had agreed to go because it would get me out of the house. All five kids at home for a whole week – it didn't bear thinking about.

"I might take the eggs with me," Danny said. "If they do hatch out into something, I want to be there when it happens."

"Just make sure the jar is screwed tight shut, then."

"But they might need oxygen. They could die without it."

I said, "If they are aliens, they might be completely different from life on earth. They might not breathe oxygen."

"That's true. They could breathe nitrogen or carbon dioxide."

"Or not breathe at all," I said. "This could be your first experiment. Keep them in the jar with the lid screwed on tight, and see if they shrivel up and die."

I really didn't believe the things were alien eggs. But I didn't think I would sleep too well on this trip if there was a chance of something slimy crawling out of Danny's backpack. (I probably wouldn't sleep too well, whatever. We were going to be sleeping on the floor of a church hall.)

In the afternoon, Rushani helped us pack up our things for the Lake District trip. There was a long list, including wet-weather gear, first aid stuff, and some chocolate for "emergency rations". I didn't like the sound of this. I was starting to wish I'd never agreed to go on the trip.

"Will we have to go for walks in the rain?" I asked Danny. "Will we have to do rock-climbing?"

"Only if you want to," he said. "There'll be a choice of things to do."

Rushani said, "Sophie went on a similar trip last year, and I'm sure she didn't go rock-climbing."

No. I couldn't imagine Sophie scrambling up a cliff – she would be afraid of chipping her nail-varnish. Sophie wasn't going on this year's trip. In fact she had stopped going to church after a huge argument with her mum.

"Ben's dad doesn't make him go to church, so why are you making me go? It's so unfair! We're supposed to be all one family now, so how come there are two sets of rules?"

I thought she had a point. Dad and Rushani were always trying to make sure we were treated equally. (It was an impossible task because we were all so different. There was always someone complaining, "That's so unfair!")

Rushani said, "But it's important to go to church, to meet with God and worship him."

"Maybe that's true, if you believe in God. But I don't – not any more. So it's a total waste of time me going to church," Sophie said. She added cunningly, "I could spend the time doing my homework."

"There are more important things than homework." (I never thought I would hear Rushani say that.)

Sophie said, "Look, Mum, I'm not a kid any more – I'm 15 years old. You can't make me believe the same as you. I'm not going to church, and that's it."

Rushani lost the argument. Sophie stopped going to church. Danny and Will still went, and sometimes Dad went too, but I guessed it was only to make Rushani happy. He didn't believe in God any more than I did.

I was hoping there wouldn't be too much religious stuff on the youth group trip. Religion was so boring. If

I had to choose between religion and rock-climbing in the pouring rain, I would pick rock-climbing, any day.

★ ★ ★

Next morning, Rushani drove us into town with all our gear. Everyone was meeting in the church car park. I saw two minibuses, their roof-racks loaded with bags. A guy called Joe – Danny said he was the youth leader – was ticking off names on a list.

There wére a few people that I vaguely recognised from school. Most of them were older than us, from Year 8 and 9. Then, to my surprise, Tom Weston arrived.

"Oh-oh," said Danny. "I was hoping he wouldn't be coming on the trip."

"Why? Tom's all right," I said. "He's in my class at school."

"He's trouble. He's always messing about at youth group. Sometimes it's funny, but mostly it's just annoying."

Tom dumped his bag at Joe's feet. He was looking sulky, as if he didn't want to be here. I went to say hi to him.

"I never knew you were coming on this trip," I said.

"My parents made me. They're going on a mini-break to Paris and they said I can't go. But what are you doing here? You don't come to youth group."

"Danny Fletcher dragged me along. He's my step-brother."

"What?" Tom stared at me. "You're Danny Fletcher's step-brother?"

"So?"

"I knew Danny at junior school. I can't stand him – he thinks he's so clever. He's the total opposite of you, Paul. It's kind of funny that you've ended up as brothers."

"Not brothers," I said. "Step-brothers."

"Do you get on all right?"

"Yeah, most of the time."

I just hoped Danny and Tom would get on all right too. If they didn't, whose side would I be on?

Oh well. It was only for four days.

★ ★ ★

It took us several hours to get to the Lake District. At last we arrived in a small village, miles from anywhere. We all spilled out of the minibus. We were surrounded by fields and hills – much bigger hills than the ones at home. There were a few houses, a tiny school, and a church. Nothing else.

"No shops?" said one of the girls, sounding shocked.

"No pub?" said a big boy, showing off.

"No lakes?" I said. "I thought this was supposed to be the Lake District."

Joe, the youth leader, laughed. "You'll see plenty of lakes. The nearest one is just a few miles away, over those fells. A fell, by the way, means a hill. A beck is a stream."

"If you think it sounds like a different language, you're right," said Mel, the other leader. "The Vikings invaded the Lake District hundreds of years ago, and those words are from their language."

I muttered to Danny, "If aliens invade the earth, I wonder what language we'll end up speaking?"

I shouldn't have said that, because it reminded him of the eggs. As soon as the luggage was unloaded, he took the jar out to see if anything had happened to them. They looked just the same as before. But Tom noticed what he was doing.

"What's that? Frogspawn?"

Danny ignored him.

"Look at this," Tom said loudly. "Danny's brought some frogspawn along with him! Are those your emergency rations, Danny?"

"The food's not going to be *that* bad," said one of the older boys.

"You hope," said another one.

Danny said, "It's not frogspawn, it's…"

His voice faded out. I could see he didn't want to talk about alien eggs – not here. The others might think he was a total nutter.

"What is it, then?" Tom asked him.

"Snake eggs," I said, thinking quickly. "He's got a pet snake. Two of them actually. Pythons."

When they heard this, some of the girls started kicking up a fuss.

"Snake eggs! Yuck!"

"Joe, come and see this! They brought snakes with them!"

Joe, the youth leader, took away the jar of jelly. "You can have it back at the end of the trip," he said to Danny. "We can't have snakes escaping, even if they're only little ones. Health and safety and all that. I'm supposed to be responsible for you lot."

He put the jar away somewhere – he wouldn't tell us where.

"Oh, great," said Danny. "I can't keep an eye on the eggs now. What if they hatch out?"

"We just have to hope the lid was screwed on tight," I said.

Chapter 9:

Genuine lakeland

I quite enjoyed the Lake District trip. We did several different activities, like rowing to an island, and exploring a forest with high-level walkways and zip lines. Another day we walked up a fell. The view from the top was awesome – mountains and lakes, and in the far distance, the sea.

All the way up the fell, Danny had kept his eyes on the ground, looking for more of the jelly stuff. But he didn't find any.

On the way back down, something happened that scared the life out of me. One minute everything was quiet and peaceful. Next minute, with a sudden huge roar that seemed to burst the sky open, something raced overhead and zoomed away down the valley.

"What was that?" I gasped, staring after it.

"A fighter plane," said one of the big boys. "It broke the sound barrier. It was going faster than the speed of sound – that's why we didn't hear it coming."

"Why would fighter planes fly around here?" Danny asked.

"The pilots do their training in remote areas like this," Joe said. "They have to practise flying close to the ground. I suppose, if a pilot makes a mistake and crashes, it wouldn't be as disastrous up here as in a city."

"Pretty disastrous for the pilot," said Tom. "Unless he managed to eject in time."

So far, Tom had been OK. I thought he might start picking on Danny, but he didn't. He went around with a couple of Year 8 boys, and didn't bother Danny or me.

In the evenings it was too dark to do outdoor things. We mostly watched DVDs and played computer games. Joe had brought along a couple of old TV sets and some games consoles. One was prehistoric – at least 20 years old. The graphics were useless, but the games were still quite playable.

Danny liked the game called (guess what?) Space Invaders. It had rows of jellyfish-like aliens descending towards earth, and you had to shoot them. That's all there was to it. Joe said it was one of the first ever computer games.

I soon got bored with it because it was so monotonous. And you couldn't really win. However many levels you got to, the aliens always destroyed you in the end.

★ ★ ★

Each night, before bedtime, there was a ten-minute religious bit. It wasn't as boring as I expected, but Tom usually got restless – just like in school. He couldn't sit there without interrupting and messing about.

On the second evening, Joe was talking about making decisions. If you had to make a choice that really mattered, one that could affect your whole life, what would help you to decide? People had lots of suggestions.

"Ask your friends what they think."

"Ask your mum and dad."

"Yes, and then do the opposite," said Tom.

A girl said, "Read your horoscope."

"Horoscopes are rubbish," said one of the boys. "Try reading your horoscope in four newspapers – you'll get four totally different forecasts."

"Yeah, forget horoscopes. Be logical. Look on the Internet, find out more information – then decide."

"The Internet can't tell you if you should ask Jade out."

"The answer's no," said Jade, and everybody laughed.

Joe said, "Any other ideas? How do we know how to make the right choice?"

"Ask God," said Tom. "That's what you want us to say, isn't it, Joe? But I always have trouble hearing the answer." He cupped his hand to his ear and frowned. "I wish God would speak up a bit."

"Sometimes it's quite easy to know what God wants us to do," said Joe, "because it's in the Bible. The Ten Commandments and the words of Jesus help us to know how God wants us to live. Like when I was at school I had a friend called Lee who used to nick things from shops. He wanted me to try it, and I nearly did because

I didn't want Lee to think I was a wimp. But then I remembered that the Bible says... well, you tell me."

"You must not steal," said one of the girls.

"Yeah. So I knew what to do. That's one way God speaks to us – through his Word, the Bible. It's like a compass when you're lost. It shows you the right way to go."

He opened up a Bible. "Listen to this prayer in the Psalms:

You are my rock and fortress,
for the sake of your name lead me and guide me."

"How can a rock lead somebody?" said Tom. "That's stupid. A rock is stuck in the same place all the time."

Joe, ignoring him, turned the page. "And this is God's promise:

I will instruct you and teach you in the way you should go;
I will counsel you and watch over you.
Don't be like the horse or the mule,
which have no understanding..."

"Did you hear that, Tom?" said one of the older boys. "Don't be like a mule."

"What's a mule?" I muttered to Danny.

"Half horse and half donkey. Very stubborn. Very stupid."

He didn't bother to keep his voice down. Tom heard him, and he gave Danny an angry look.

Danny might be clever in school, but he wasn't that smart at understanding other people. He said things without thinking. Maybe he didn't realise that he could upset people. Maybe he didn't care.

* * *

Next day we visited a town by a lake, to do something Joe called a treasure hunt. He split us into four teams and gave us a list of things we had to find out before lunchtime. Danny read them out to our team.

Some of them sounded quite easy. What was the name of the local school? When was the last bus to Penrith that night? Which shop sold the cheapest postcards?

Others sounded harder. What was Aira Force? (Clue: nothing at all to do with planes.) Which famous writer was buried in the churchyard? Where would you find cat bells?

"Cat bells? In a pet shop, obviously," said Jade.

"It's a trick question," Danny said. "Catbells is the name of a hill. And I think Aira Force is a waterfall."

"How do you know?"

"I just happened to read a bit about the Lake District before we came."

"Danny's so intelligent," Tom said. "Brain the size of a planet... memory like an elephant. Isn't that right, Danny?"

"Shut up, Tom." Danny looked annoyed.

Trying to avoid a row, I took the list and read out the next question. "How much is it for... er... dangers and mash at the Lake Café?"

"Dangers and mash?" Danny looked down at the list. "It doesn't say *dangers*, it says *bangers*. Bangers and mash. Look, don't bother, Paul. I'll read it out – you listen."

He made me feel like a 4-year-old. *I'm not dumb, I'm dyslexic, that's all,* I wanted to tell the others. I could see they were trying not to laugh. Dangers and mash!

We had been told to stick together. But as Danny and the others charged off down the street, I lagged behind. I had stopped caring about the stupid treasure hunt.

Tom dropped back to join me. He said, "I don't want to do this either. It's totally pointless. Let's find something else to do."

But there wasn't much to do in the small town. We wandered round a few shops full of tourist things. Tea-towels covered in Lakeland poetry. Clocks made of genuine Lakeland slate. And slabs of some stuff called Kendal Mint Cake, which was pearly white, almost see-through.

"That looks a bit like those egg things of Danny's," said Tom. "What are they, anyway? Don't say snake eggs... I know you made that up."

I wouldn't have told him if I hadn't been annoyed with Danny. "He thinks they're alien eggs. We found them on the moor."

"Alien eggs! You can't be serious."

"Well, what do you think they are? Nobody seems to know."

"Haven't a clue. But alien eggs! If he really thinks that, he's crazy. And why did he bring them on the trip?"

"He thought they might hatch while we were away."

"He's mad," said Tom. "You've got a lunatic for a step-brother. You'd better hope it's not catching."

We went into a few more shops. I bought some genuine Lakeland fudge to take home. Tom bought some Kendal Mint Cake, and something else which he wouldn't show me.

Then we wandered down to the lake shore, hoping to hire a motorboat. But they were quite expensive, and the man told us we were too young.

"Maybe we could just, like, borrow a boat," Tom said to me. "Look, there's one that nobody's using."

He pointed to a rowing boat that lay further along the shore. Going closer, we saw that the oars had been left in it.

"Careless," said Tom. "That's like leaving your car unlocked with the key inside. Why don't we take it out on the lake?"

"Don't be daft," I said. "The owner might see us."

"What if he does?"

"You'll get in trouble," I warned him.

"Why? I'm not nicking it, just borrowing it. I'll bring it back all right. Go on, Paul, it'll be a laugh. Anyway, what else is there to do in this dump?"

In the end he persuaded me. After all, the boat was just sitting there. The only person who might see us take it was the man in charge of the hire-boats, and he was reading the paper.

We took off our shoes and had a paddle in the lake, like 5-year-olds. When we were close to the boat, we grabbed the sides of it and slid it into the water. Then we climbed in and started rowing, one oar on each side. We were quite good at this as long as we kept in time with each other.

"Hey! That's my boat!" A man was running along the shore, waving his arms and shouting. "What do you think you're doing?"

But by this time we were out in deep water. Tom was laughing his head off. Typical – he never cared about what might happen next.

"He can't catch us. Not unless he's an Olympic swimmer," Tom said. "Come on, let's make for that island."

I felt uneasy. I just knew we wouldn't get away with this.

The man had stopped chasing us. He was talking to the guy in charge of the hire-boats. A minute later we heard the sound of a motor starting up.

"He's coming after us in a motorboat!" I gasped.

"Oh-oh. Pirates on the starboard bow. Maybe we'd better head for the shore."

Our rowing went to pieces as we frantically turned the boat around and aimed for the nearest land. This was a wooded headland sticking out into the water. The boat bumped against some rocks. We leaped out and ran into the trees.

Luckily for us, the owner didn't chase us. He was more bothered about getting his boat back. We hurried through the woods until we came to a road leading back into town. I had lost my socks, and my trainers were soaking wet.

"I told you it was a crazy thing to do," I said to Tom.

He grinned. "It was a laugh, though, wasn't it? More fun than a stupid treasure hunt."

We got back to the minibus just as the others were arriving.

"Where did you get to?" Danny asked me.

"Nowhere much," I said.

★ ★ ★

That night it was our turn to help with the washing-up. Tom was putting things away in the kitchen cupboard, when he suddenly said, "Hey, Danny, want to know where Joe hid those snake eggs of yours? Up there, look."

We could just see the jar, half-hidden behind some dusty vases on the top shelf. Danny had a quick look around. Joe was nowhere in sight.

Danny climbed up on the worktop and reached into the cupboard. The moment he brought the jar out, I could see there was something different about it – different colours. Yellow and green things were mixed in with the white eggs.

"I don't believe it," Danny gasped. "They've hatched!"

Chapter 10:

Yellow and green

"Those don't look like snakes," said Si, one of the other boys.

"That's because they're not snakes. They're aliens," said Danny.

There were 10 or 12 strange shapes, a bit like small slugs, no bigger than my thumbnail. Bright yellow and acid green, they lay unmoving among the blobs of white jelly.

"Aliens?" said Si doubtfully. "But they're tiny."

"A human embryo is even smaller than that," said Danny. "These are newly hatched. We don't know how big they could grow."

"What are you going to do with them?" I asked him.

He didn't answer. He turned the jar around, gazing at the strange objects. They were fat at one end, slim at the other, with no visible eyes or ears or anything. There was nothing threatening about them, but they made me feel uneasy. Were they really from another planet?

"What makes you think they're aliens?" asked a girl called Lauren.

Danny launched into the story of the UFO, and our discovery of the eggs on the moor.

"It looks to me as if the aliens are seeding the earth with their eggs," he said. "It's like a secret invasion. They've probably left them in lots of different places."

"So you think they're dangerous?" said Si.

"If they are, we won't know until it's too late," said Tom. "Until there are thousands of them, an army of huge green and yellow slug things, attacking London and New York. Leaving trails of slime as wide as a motorway. Eating everything in their path."

"You've been watching too many movies," I said.

"Let's have a look," said Tom, and Danny passed him the jar. He started unscrewing the lid.

"No!" cried Danny. "Don't let them out!"

Tom said, "We ought to destroy them. It's the safest thing to do."

He took out one of the yellow things, looked at it for a second, and then popped it into his mouth! Lauren screamed.

"You idiot!" Danny shouted. "Spit it out. It could be a parasite that eats you up from inside!"

Tom chewed and swallowed. "It didn't taste too bad actually. I think I'll have another one."

Danny snatched the jar away from him. I thought of that movie where a creature grows inside a man's stomach, and then comes bursting out, splattering everyone with alien goo. Could that happen to Tom?

Lauren was still screaming. Joe came running in.

"What's going on?"

"We have to get Tom to hospital," Danny said, his face white. "He's just eaten an alien creature. It could poison him, or kill him."

Tom was looking very strange. For a minute I thought he was about to be sick. Then I realised he was trying not to laugh. Like an alien erupting through his stomach wall, the laughter burst out uncontrollably.

"He... he... actually believed me," Tom gasped. "He thinks they're aliens. But they're sweets! I put them there. Look!"

He pulled a bag out of his pocket. It was half-full of yellow and green things, exactly like the ones in the jar. He handed the bag around.

"Have an alien. Go on – help yourself," he said.

As people realised what had happened, they started laughing too... all except Danny. He was bright red with embarrassment.

Everyone hates being laughed at – even clever people. It's probably worse for clever people, because they're not used to it. Danny would hardly speak to me all evening. He seemed to be blaming me for what had happened.

"It was nothing to do with me," I told him. "I had no idea what Tom was planning to do."

"How did Tom know that I thought the eggs came from aliens? You must have told him."

"Oh. Yeah, I suppose I did. Sorry, Danny... I never meant him to trick you like that."

He wasn't listening. He walked away.

I felt really bad. I knew Danny and I could never be like brothers, but we had started to be friends. Now that

68

was all messed up, and it was my fault. Or partly my fault.

"He'll get over it," said Tom.

"You don't know Danny too well if you think that. He doesn't forget things."

"Oh yeah... memory like an elephant. I forgot that." He grinned at me. "It was funny, though, wasn't it? His face!"

"It was dumb," I said.

"Come on, Paul, lighten up a bit. How about a quick game of Space Invaders?"

★ ★ ★

Joe's talk that night was about David and Goliath. He showed us a newspaper article that mentioned those names from the day when Mallenford United took on Chelsea in the Cup. (No one was surprised that Mallenford lost 6–0.)

I hadn't realised that the original David and Goliath were people in the Bible. David was a young shepherd. His older brothers were soldiers in King Saul's army, but David was too young to fight.

David was sent to take supplies to his brothers. He found the soldiers on a hillside, with their enemies, the Philistines, on the opposite hill. And in the valley between, a huge man, over nine feet tall, was striding to and fro.

He was Goliath, the Philistines' champion. He was shouting insults and calling on King Saul to send out a champion to fight him. But nobody dared to go, not even the king. Goliath's spear was as thick as a gatepost. His weapons and armour weighed as much as a full-grown man.

David said, "Who is this Philistine who's insulting the soldiers of the Living God? If nobody else will fight him, I will!"

His big brothers laughed and told him not to be an idiot. "Run back home to your sheep," they said. But someone told King Saul about the young shepherd who wasn't afraid of Goliath. David was brought before the king.

"You can't possibly fight that giant," King Saul told him. "He's a man of war. You're only a young lad!"

"Sir, when I was looking after sheep, I had to face up to lions and bears," David said. "I managed to kill them and rescue my sheep. God, who saved me from the paws of animals, will save me from Goliath, too."

His words and his bravery impressed King Saul. "Go and fight him, then," he said, "and may God be with you."

David could have worn the king's armour and carried the king's sword, but they weighed him down too much. He went out to meet the giant, carrying only his shepherd's stick, his sling and a bag with five smooth round stones in it.

Goliath couldn't believe what he was seeing. He laughed at David.

"So you think I'm a dog, do you? You want to fight me with a stick? Come here. I'm going to feed you to the vultures!"

★ ★ ★

Joe stopped telling the story for a minute. He looked round at all of us.

He said, "By now, David must have got quite used to people mocking him and looking down on him. First his brothers, then the king, and now Goliath... they all told him he couldn't possibly win. But he didn't let them put him off. What was his secret?"

"He trusted in God," said Lauren.

"That's right. Remember that psalm-prayer that I read the other night? It was David who wrote those words. To him, God was like a rock and a fortress. If you're in a castle on a rock, scornful words can't do you any harm.

"David called out to Goliath, *You come against me with sword and spear, but I come against you in the name of the Lord Almighty. Everyone will see that God doesn't save by sword and spear. But the battle is the Lord's, and he will give you into our hands.*

"Then he ran towards Goliath, and as he ran, he put a stone in his sling, aimed it and let it fly. All Goliath's armour couldn't save him. The stone hit him in the middle of the forehead, and he fell flat on the ground.

"David took Goliath's own sword and used it to cut his head off. And when the Philistines saw that Goliath was dead, they all ran away. David had trusted in God, his rock and his fortress, and God hadn't let him down."

It was a good story and even Tom had listened, although at the end he said, "Mallenford United made one big mistake, I reckon. They should have taken a few slings and stones onto the pitch with them."

"They still would have lost," said Si, who was a Chelsea supporter.

Later, lying in my sleeping bag, I wondered what it would be like to believe in the God of the Bible. It must be good to think that there was someone looking after you. Someone strong, who was always there, who would never leave you unprotected – like a rock, like a fortress.

Joe believed in this God, and so did Rushani. But to me, God felt as unreal as Danny's aliens. I couldn't start to believe in him just because other people did. Was he really there, somewhere out in space?

God, if you really exist, prove it to me somehow, I found myself praying in the darkness.

But nothing happened. No flash of light, no voice inside my head. No sound at all, apart from other people snoring. After a long time I drifted off to sleep.

Chapter 11:

Space Wars

When we got home from the trip, Danny still wasn't speaking to me. I think Dad and Rushani had hoped the trip would make us more friendly, but it had done exactly the opposite.

It's awkward sharing a bedroom with somebody who totally ignores you. Danny acted as if he was the only person in the room, or rather in his corner of it. He had a sort of invisible line around his bed and his belongings. If any of my things crossed that line, he kicked them back onto my side.

This annoyed me. When he wasn't there, I crossed the invisible line and messed up a few of his things. Nothing too mean – I didn't damage anything. I just put his DVDs in the wrong cases and his books in different boxes, stuff like that. He was a very tidy person, unlike me, and he soon noticed.

He couldn't ask me if I'd done it because he wasn't talking to me. But when everyone was there, he said, "Somebody's been messing about with my books and DVDs. Who was it?"

"Not me," said Sophie.

"Why would I touch your stupid DVDs?" asked Ben.

I said, "It was probably Will."

"I never!" said Will. "But somebody broke my Lego house. When I find out who did it I'll kill them!"

This made me laugh. He was only 4, after all. But even little kids can be quite dangerous if they want to be.

Things a 4-year-old could do to a full-grown man:
– Run out in front of his car and cause a crash.
– Make him read *Thomas the Tank Engine* 10,000 times.
– Leave toys at top of stairs for him to trip over.
–Wake him up at least three times every night (make that 13 times on the night before a birthday).
– Refuse to eat anything except Coco Pops, then (when the cupboard is full of Coco Pops) change over to Frosted Shreddies.
– Nick his lighter and try to set his wellies on fire.
– Swop his blood pressure pills for Smarties.
– Find where he hid a box of posh chocolates, take bites out of most of them and put them back.
– Eat his winning lottery ticket.
– Run along a crowded street, screaming, "That man's trying to make me get in his car!"

Will had actually tried a couple of these on Dad. The box of chocolates had been meant as a present for Rushani, but Dad had to throw it away. The wellies, luckily, didn't catch fire – the rubber just melted a bit and gave off a horrible smell. The lottery ticket was only worth £10, but even if it had been worth £10 million, Dad wouldn't have done much. He would have let

Rushani tell Will off because Will was Rushani's son, not his.

Using this system, Dad told me off for not getting on better with Danny. (I guessed Rushani was having the same conversation with Danny about me.) I tried to explain that it wasn't really my fault.

"I did say sorry, but he wouldn't listen. He's not talking to me. What am I supposed to do?"

"I don't know," Dad said, and he sighed.

I said, "Life would be so much easier if families didn't exist. If we all lived on our own, like trees."

"Don't say that. There are some good things about families."

"Oh yeah? Dad, at this moment I can't think of a single one."

★ ★ ★

One Sunday morning I was surprised to see Ben, in his dressing gown, coming out of Sophie's room.

"Sophie's not here," Ben explained. "She's staying over at a friend's house."

"I bet she won't like you sleeping in her bed," I said.

"*Her* bed? *My* bed, don't you mean?" he said. "I'm sick of sleeping in the office. There's no room to stretch your legs out. Anyway, Sophie isn't going to know, is she?"

But she did know, because Ben had left a dirty sock under the bed. Sophie found it when she was unpacking her things.

"Who's been sleeping in my room?" she demanded.

Will giggled. "You sound like the Three Bears. Who's been eating my porridge? Who's been sleeping in my bed?"

"I bet it was you, Ben. It smells like you." Sophie threw the sock at him. "Disgusting!"

Ben said, "What about how you've made my room smell, all sickly sweet and girly? And it's *my* room, Sophie, not yours. I let you borrow it because Dad said I had to, but I want it back now. You can sleep in the office for a change."

Sophie said, "I can't sleep there! Where will I put all my clothes and things?"

"Same place as I've had to put mine. In heaps all around the room."

"Yes, but your clothes are used to that kind of treatment," said Sophie. "And you only possess three T-shirts and two pairs of jeans."

"You've got far more clothes than you could ever wear," said Ben. "You ought to get rid of half of them. Why have you still got that fluffy ballet outfit that says *Age 7*?"

"You've been looking through my wardrobe!" Sophie cried, outraged.

"Don't you mean *my* wardrobe? Anyway, I want my room back. I'll give you two days to get out."

They had a huge row, ending in Sophie storming off to get Rushani on her side, and Ben complaining to Dad. *It's so unfair!* could be heard loudly from two different rooms.

I thought Ben was in the right. For weeks he'd put up with sleeping on an air bed in a cramped space the size of a bathroom. (In fact, there was more room in the bathroom than the office, if you didn't mind sleeping in the bath.) Why shouldn't Sophie take a turn at doing that? It was our house, after all.

I had a sudden thought that made me laugh out loud.

"What's so funny?" asked Will.

"Space invaders. That's what you lot are."

"What do you mean?"

"You and your family – you're like aliens from the planet Zarg. Taking over our world. Invading our space and making us obey your weird customs."

"What weird customs?" Danny said, then looked annoyed at himself for speaking to me.

"Oh, you know… keeping things tidy. Eating at a table instead of in front of the TV. Doing homework before you absolutely have to. Putting dirty socks in the wash instead of on the floor… all that stuff."

These were all things that Rushani was keen on. And Dad backed her up, even though he never used to bother much about them before. He liked the tidy house, the ironed shirts, and Rushani's delicious cooking, which was a mixture of English and Sri Lankan style food. I liked all these things too, but I missed the freedom of the old days B.I. (Before Invasion).

I wondered how Dad and Rushani would sort out the quarrel about the bedrooms. But Rushani came up with an answer.

"Whoever agrees to sleep in the office will get first choice of the new bedrooms, when they are ready. Why don't we all go and look to see how the workmen are getting on?"

It was a Sunday, so the workmen weren't there. Dad moved aside the piece of wood that was acting as a door into the barn, and we all went in.

Quite a lot had been done since the last time I looked. All the rooms had floors and walls now, and some had doors. You could see the shape of the huge new kitchen and dining area. There was also a utility room.

"Lots of space for muddy shoes," Rushani said happily. "No more mud in my kitchen."

On the next floor we could see a bathroom and three new bedrooms, one with its own shower room. None were finished, but they all looked as if they might be ready by Christmas, with a bit of luck.

Sophie said, "If I can choose the bedroom with the shower, I'll move into the office for now."

Everyone seemed happy with this. If Sophie got her own shower, the rest of us might have a chance of getting into a bathroom now and then.

I wanted to look at the attic room, but the workmen hadn't built any stairs yet. There was only a ladder going up from the landing.

"Can we go up there?" asked Ben.

"All right, but be careful," Dad said.

"Not you, Will," Rushani said. "You stay down here."

Ben, Sophie, Danny and I climbed up the ladder and looked around.

"Wow!" said Sophie, her voice echoing in the emptiness. "Great place for a party."

The attic room was enormous. There was definitely space for a pool table. Only one problem – there was no way of getting it in, unless a crane lowered it through a roof window.

I was just planning where my drum kit would go, when Sophie yelled, "Will! Get down!"

Will, grinning all over his face, climbed off the top step of the ladder. I could hear Rushani shouting at him from below, telling him to come down. He ignored her totally.

"I like this room," he said. "Can this be my bedroom?"

"No," we all told him, and Danny added, "You won't even be allowed in here."

"Why not?"

"Because we don't want you messing around with our things. Go on, get out of here."

He tried to catch Will, but the kid was too quick for him. He dodged aside and ran round the room. "Can't catch me!" he yelled, looking back to see if Danny was gaining on him.

There were no railings around the opening where the staircase would be fitted. Will was running so fast that he didn't see the danger. Sophie cried out and tried to stop him, but too late.

He fell right through the gap. I will never forget the sound of his scream.

Chapter 12:

Blame

We all scrambled down the ladder. Rushani was leaning over Will, who lay quite still. For one horrible moment, I thought the fall had killed him.

"He's alive," Rushani said. "He's breathing. Don't touch him! We must not move him until the ambulance gets here."

"Why not?" I asked.

"In case he has damaged his spine. Moving him could make it worse."

I looked at Will's small body, lying crumpled on the floor. I'd always thought he was an annoying little brat, but now, seeing him hurt and helpless, I had to feel sorry for him.

There was a man in Mallenford who had been knocked off a motorbike. Now he had brain damage. He couldn't speak except for swear words. He spent his days sitting in the park, cursing and swearing.

What if Will was brain-damaged? What if his neck was broken and he ended up in a wheelchair?

Dad had called for an ambulance straight away. But because we lived out of town, it might take some time to arrive. Dad sent Ben to the end of our road, in case the ambulance missed the turning and drove past.

Now all we could do was wait. Rushani sat on the floor, stroking Will's hand. I thought she was being incredibly calm – then I saw tears rolling down her cheeks.

Sophie was getting into a state. "Where's the ambulance? Why aren't they here yet?" She paced up and down like a restless tiger in a cage. "Why do we have to live in this useless place? I told you we should never have come here!"

"Sophie," Dad said, "you're not helping."

She swore at him. I thought he would get mad at her, but he didn't. He asked her to fetch a blanket for Will. She brought back two, one for her mum. It was cold in here – almost as cold as outdoors.

And still we had to wait.

"Isn't there anything we can do, Mum?" Danny asked.

"We can pray," said Rushani. "That is all we can do right now."

So we all prayed for Will. I think even Sophie was praying. Please let him be OK... please make the ambulance come quickly...

By now it was getting dark. We couldn't switch the lights on because there weren't any. Dad sent me to get a torch. Just as I came back with it, the ambulance arrived.

It seemed to take ages to get Will into the ambulance. He was strapped onto a stretcher, still unconscious, with his head in a sort of box thing to keep his neck straight.

Then Rushani got into the ambulance, and it drove away slowly down our rutted drive.

There wasn't room for Dad in the ambulance, but he wanted to be with Rushani. He got into his car to drive to the hospital. Sophie asked if she could go too, but Dad said Will would probably be in intensive care. He wouldn't be allowed many visitors.

"I'll ring you as soon as we know anything," Dad said.

We went indoors to a house that felt empty and dead. Danny was being even quieter than before. Since Will's fall, he had hardly said a word to anyone.

Sophie sat down next to him and put her arm around his shoulders. This was such an un-Sophie-like thing to do that I couldn't help staring.

"It wasn't your fault," she said to Danny. "Nobody will blame you."

He stared at the floor.

Sophie said, "Will's not going to die. He isn't! He'll be absolutely fine in a few days. Running around annoying everybody as usual."

I really hoped she was right.

★ ★ ★

Dad rang a couple of hours later. Will was conscious again, but in a lot of pain. He would have to stay in hospital for now, so that the doctors could keep him under observation. Rushani was going to stay overnight – there were beds where parents could sleep.

Dad came home late that evening. He hadn't eaten, so I made him an omelette. I had done the same for the others, earlier. This was the first time I'd cooked anything for ages, and I realised that I'd been missing it.

Danny didn't eat much, but Sophie was quite impressed. "I never knew you could cook like this, Paul. How did you learn?"

"We had to learn after Mum left," I said. "You were lucky. You still had your mum."

"Mums can't do everything," she said. "My theory is, mums are good at looking after people, but dads are better at making them do what they're told. Like Will only obeys Mum when he feels like it."

"Yeah, we noticed," said Ben.

I said to Danny, "If Will had done what your mum told him to, none of this would have happened. It's Will's fault, not yours."

Danny looked angry. He said to Sophie, "You see? People *are* going to blame me."

He spent the rest of the evening in our room, pretending to read a book. (I've done that often enough myself to know when people are pretending. They turn the pages now and then, but their eyes don't move.)

When it was bedtime, it felt very strange not to have Will there. We usually had to step carefully around his mattress, trying not to wake him. If he did wake up, he could be a real pest – but that night I wouldn't have minded.

Usually Rushani pulled the curtains when she put Will to bed. Danny, half-undressed, suddenly realised they were still open, and he hurried to close them.

"You needn't bother," I said. "There isn't another house within half a mile of here."

"Then how come I can see a light?"

He was staring out of the back window. Normally, all you could see from there was trees. But he was right. There was a small light out there, and it was moving. Someone was out in the woods with a torch.

"It's nearly midnight. What on earth are they doing?" he said, half to himself.

I put the bedroom light out so that we could see better. The torchlight was still there, but it had stopped moving. It couldn't be far inside the wood, or the trees would have hidden it.

"Sometimes there are poachers in those woods," I said. "They come after the deer."

"Poachers wouldn't show a light, though, would they?"

As he said it, the light went out. We watched for a while, but it didn't come on again. It was quite creepy to think of someone standing there in the darkness and silence. What were they doing? Were they watching our house?

I went downstairs to make sure the doors were locked. In the old days we sometimes forgot to do that, which had horrified Rushani. She always checked. But she wasn't here tonight.

Danny was in bed when I got back. I could tell he was still awake by the sound of his breathing.

"You know something? I miss your mum," I said to him.

"You're not the only one."

His voice sounded flat and depressed. But at least he was talking to me again.

I said, "I even miss Will. I never thought I'd say that."

"Yeah."

He was silent for a minute. Then he said, "It *was* my fault, you know."

"No it wasn't. He shouldn't have even been there."

"But when I was chasing him, I could see where he was heading, and just for a split second, I actually *wanted* him to fall down that hole."

"Don't feel so bad! It's not like you pushed him over the edge."

"Pushed him, chased him... What's the difference?"

I said, "I nearly killed Ben once. We were fighting over this go-kart in the garden, and I hit him with Dad's spade. There was blood everywhere. Ben's still got the scar."

"Was your dad angry with you?"

"Well, yes. But when he knew Ben was going to be OK, he calmed down. He said that's what brothers are for – to toughen each other up."

"But if Will's not OK..." Danny said, and then he stopped. I waited, saying nothing.

After a minute he went on, "If Will's not OK, I don't think Mum will ever get over it. She'll always hate me. Because Will's her favourite child."

"What makes you think that? I'd say she always tries to treat everybody the same."

"Yeah, she *tries* to, but Will gets away with loads of things I was never allowed to do. It's been like that ever since he was born. You know you called us space invaders? That's what it felt like when Will arrived. He invaded my space. He took over the whole house. Suddenly we couldn't go anywhere or do anything because of this *baby*." He almost spat the word out.

"So you've never got on with him, ever since he was born?"

"You could say that, yeah. We've always fought and argued. And Mum's always on his side."

"Because he's little," I said. "Not because she loves him more than you."

But I could tell he didn't believe me. And he still felt guilty. Nothing I could say made any difference to that.

Chapter 13:

Sticky

Next morning, in the frantic rush to get ready for school – even more frantic without Rushani – I forgot about the light we'd seen in the woods. Coming back on the bus, Danny reminded me about it.

"We could have a look around," he said. "See if there are any clues about who was there and why."

"What about cooking supper?" I said, but Ben surprised us both by offering to do it.

"If I can remember how," he added.

The house was empty when we got home. That was how it always used to be in the old days. But now I missed Rushani welcoming us home and asking how the day had gone.

That lost, lonely look was on Danny's face again. Trying to take his mind off things, I said, "Do you still want to go into the woods? Then we ought to go now. We don't have much time before dark."

The woods were not fenced off because they were common land. Anybody could go there, and in daylight you sometimes met people walking their dogs. Not now, though – it was too close to nightfall. Long shadows lay between the leafless trees.

There were muddy paths here and there. We saw a few human footprints, and deer prints too. In one place we even found motorbike tyre marks.

"You'd have to be crazy to ride a motorbike here," said Danny.

"He didn't ride it, he pushed it," I said, pointing to the footprints alongside the wheel marks.

Then, up the hill directly above our house, we came on a kind of shelter made from branches. It was like a grown-up version of the dens that Ben and I used to build. It looked as if it might even keep the rain out.

There were tyre marks here, too. You could see a place where a motorbike had stood for a while, its wheels sinking deeper into the mud.

"Why would anyone choose to build a den here?" asked Danny.

"I don't know. To go bird-watching? To look for foxes or deer?"

"Or maybe to watch for UFOs," said Danny.

"Why would they come here to do that? Did you tell anyone about the one we saw?"

"Only a few million people on the Internet. And I told Mr Martin at school."

"Oh yeah... you were going to show him the eggs," I said. "What did he think of them?"

"He said it would be hard to analyse them. They're contaminated with green and yellow food colouring. He said I should try and get some more."

"I could help you look for some." I didn't really want to, but maybe it would help to make up for the ones that

Tom had messed up. "Not right now, though. It's nearly dark."

Before we left, I smashed up the shelter. I didn't like to think of someone – maybe more than one person – hiding out in the woods so close to our house. I kicked away the wooden supports, and the roof fell in.

Back home, a good smell was coming from the kitchen. As we went in, Ben threw a strand of spaghetti at the wall, where it stuck like a snail on a flowerpot.

"Why did you do that?" asked Danny.

"If it sticks, that means it's cooked."

"What's wrong with using a timer? Or a clock?"

"Look, kid, do you want to take over?" said Ben, annoyed. "I bet you can't even boil an egg."

Sophie said to Danny, "Mum rang. She says they'll probably let Will come home tomorrow."

"So he's all right, then?" I said.

"He's still got a sore head, but he hasn't got concussion or anything. Mum thinks it's an answer to prayer. I say it's because he's got a thick skull."

Danny said nothing, but he suddenly looked very happy.

★ ★ ★

The next few nights were cloudy. Although we looked out each night at bedtime, we never saw the moving light in the woods.

Danny said, "That proves it. He must be looking for UFOs. If he was studying owls or badgers or whatever, cloudy weather wouldn't stop him."

"I don't see why he should think a UFO would come back to the same place twice," I said.

"Because that's what they do. There are some areas where a lot of UFOs are seen – often in places where there are prehistoric burial mounds and stone circles."

"What have those got to do with UFOs?"

"Some people think that aliens have been visiting the earth for centuries. They could have helped primitive people to build things like Stonehenge, or the Pyramids, or the Nazca Lines in Peru."

"What on earth for?"

"Nobody knows."

"There's a stone circle up on the moor," I said. "Not a very big one. I mean it's not like Stonehenge or anything. It's just a few old rocks on top of a hill."

"I wouldn't mind having a look at it," said Danny. "And we might find some eggs on the way."

"OK, we'll go at the weekend."

"Can I go too?" said Will.

I could tell Danny wanted to say no, but he was trying to be nice to Will since he came out of hospital. (The fall didn't seem to have harmed Will at all, apart from giving him a black eye. He looked as if he'd been in a fight.)

I said, "It's a long way, Will. You wouldn't be able to walk that far. Maybe when you're a bit bigger…"

"That's so unfair! I never get to do anything! Everybody always says I'm too little!"

"I don't know why you're so keen to go up on the moor," I said. "It's a pretty boring place. Nothing except hills and sheep."

"And marshy places," said Danny. "You could sink down into the marsh and never be seen again, Will."

That shut him up for a while. But on Saturday, when we were putting our boots on, Will started whingeing on about it again. When we said he couldn't go with us, he went running to Rushani.

"Mum! Make Danny take me too!"

"No, Will, you're too little. You stay with me and we'll do something nice. Would you like to help me make some cakes?"

"I don't want to do cooking! I'm not a girl! I want to go with the big boys."

"I wouldn't mind learning how to make cakes," I said, because that was something I'd never been good at. The few times I tried, they were disastrous, burnt on top or soggy in the middle.

Dad said, "I tell you what, Will, you come out and help me clean the car. You can hold the hose, as long as you don't spray me."

Clean the car? He hardly ever bothered because our drive was so muddy. As soon as the car went out again, it would look as if it hadn't been cleaned for weeks. But then I saw what he was doing – trying to get more involved with Will, instead of leaving Rushani to deal with him.

It worked. Will went out quite happily to clean the car. But as we went up the hill, Danny said, "You see? Will really is Mum's favourite."

"Are you saying that because she made him stay at home? She would be just as worried about you, if you'd half-killed yourself falling out of the attic."

"I don't think so," he said.

When people are really convinced about something, it's hard to change their minds. I thought that if Rushani had made us take Will with us, Danny would still have called it favouritism. It was a no-win situation.

"Ever thought of how Will looks at things?" I said. "He probably thinks *you're* the favourite. You can do lots of things he's not allowed to do."

"Are you on Will's side too?" Danny said angrily.

"No. I'm on your side."

We passed the place where the shelter had been. There was no sign that anyone had tried to rebuild it. There had been a lot of rain recently, and the motorbike tracks had almost been washed away.

Without wasting any time there, we went out onto the open moor. We had the compass, and a map that showed where the stone circle was. I had only been there once. It was a couple of miles to the north, on the highest point of the moor. There were no roads – the only way to get there was by walking across country.

We soon found out that it wasn't going to be easy. The autumn rain had made the marshy ground even wetter than last time. Our compass pointed us in the right direction, but often the marshes got in the way.

After we'd made several long detours, Danny decided to go straight across the next bit of bog. He wanted to road-test his new wellies, he said.

"You'll get stuck," I warned him, but he wouldn't listen.

"Come on," he called to me, squelching through the mud. "It's quite shallow, really. Oh!"

One foot had suddenly gone in much deeper. The mud came over the top of his left boot. When he pulled his foot out, the boot was left behind. Balancing on the other leg, he tried to tug his boot free, but this only made his right foot sink deeper in.

"Come back," I shouted.

"I... I can't," he gasped. "I'm stuck! I can't move!"

Chapter 14:

Help us!

I took a few steps towards Danny. But because I was taller and heavier, I felt my feet sinking before I got anywhere near him. Hastily I got back onto solid ground.

"Just forget about your boots," I told him. "Leave them, and get back here."

But he couldn't move. The mud was above his knees now, and his struggles were making him sink in deeper. How deep could the marsh be? Would he really sink right down and be swallowed up?

I could see fear on his face. I was starting to panic too.

I looked around for help. We were in a valley between low hills, and there was no one in sight – nothing moving except for sheep. Danny had a phone, but it was useless out here where the signal was so bad.

"I'll go back and get help," I said.

"Be quick, then. I'm scared, Paul!"

I started running back the way we had come. As I ran, I was praying. Don't let Danny sink any deeper... Help me to find the way home... Oh, God, please help us...

I began to wonder if I would ever be able to find Danny again, out here where all the hills and valleys looked alike. I looked around, trying to fix things in my memory. A bent tree. A heap of rocks. A flat-topped hill.

Wait a minute. There was someone on the hilltop – a man walking alone.

"Help! Help!" I shouted.

The man heard me. He hurried down the hill, and I ran to meet him. Suddenly I realised who he was… Mr Martin, our science teacher.

"What's wrong?"

"Danny Fletcher. He's stuck in the marsh," I gasped.

"Where?"

"Over there. In the next valley."

We ran back. I was wondering if Mr Martin would actually be much help. He wasn't very tall or strong-looking.

He stopped suddenly as we passed a tree. There was a fallen branch on the ground, and he picked it up. Why hadn't I thought of that?

The branch wasn't long enough to reach Danny. Mr Martin had to go a few steps into the marsh before he could hold it out far enough. Danny grabbed the end of it like a lifeline. By now the mud was halfway up his thighs.

"Don't be afraid," said Mr Martin. "You cannot sink right down beneath the surface. Your body is lighter than the mud. When people die in places like this, it's because they starve to death, or because the tide comes in and drowns them." He looked around. "And we have plenty of time before the tide comes in."

Was that meant as a joke? I didn't think of Mr Martin as a joker. But Danny, much less frightened now, was actually smiling.

"Hold on and don't let go," Mr Martin said. "Are you ready?"

He gave a mighty heave. With a horrible squelching, sucking noise, the mud let go of its grip on Danny's legs. He came slithering towards us, pulled along by the branch. Mr Martin must be a lot stronger than he looked.

"My boots," he said. "I've lost my boots."

"Never mind them. You'll have to go home in your socks," I said.

His legs and feet were totally covered in reddish-brown mud. He was shivering, and his brand new boots were gone for ever. But he was safe – that was the main thing.

Mr Martin was pretty muddy, too. He went into teacher mode for a minute, telling us off for taking risks. Then he walked back with us to the edge of the moor. We both thanked him for his help.

"It is fortunate that I was there at the right time," he said.

"What were you doing on the moor?" Danny asked him. "Just taking a walk?"

"I was looking for some of that jelly-like substance that you showed me. And I have found some." He took a plastic bag out of his pocket. It was full of the white egg things.

He said, "I think we might examine this in Science Club on Thursday. I wonder if anyone will work out what it is? I have some ideas. You should come along, Danny."

When we were in sight of home, Mr Martin said goodbye.

"Are you going to walk all the way back to town?" Danny asked him.

"No. I have left my bike at the edge of the woods."

I thought he meant a bicycle. But before we reached our door, we heard the sound of a motorbike starting up.

"He's got a motorbike!" I said to Danny.

"So? Is there any rule that says teachers can't have them?"

"That's not what I meant. I was thinking about the watcher in the woods."

Danny stared at me. "You don't mean it was Mr Martin? Don't be stupid. Give me one good reason why he would do that."

I could think of several things he could have been doing.

- Studying animals, birds and so on. (he was a science teacher, after all).
- Practising survival techniques for an Amazon expedition (teachers have to do something in the long summer holidays).
- Keeping an eye on our house, making plans to break in (teachers don't get paid enough).
- Getting away from it all, communing with nature (teachers are under a lot of stress).
- Looking out for an alien spaceship (teachers are weird... quite a few of them could be aliens in disguise).

"I told you before that he was an alien," I said. "And look how he managed to pull you out of the marsh. Superhuman strength, see? And then there's the way he talks."

"Like a foreigner, you mean? That's because he *is* a foreigner. He's from somewhere in Eastern Europe, I think. He changed his name to Martin because no one over here could say his real name."

"He's using a false name!" This gave me another idea. "Maybe he's a spy – you know, like in a Bond movie. Maybe the UFO isn't from outer space. It's from the air force base at Murrayhill... they're testing a new kind of weapon. And he's spying on it."

"You don't like him much, do you?"

"He doesn't like me much, either. You notice he didn't invite me to his Science Club. But I think I'll go along anyway, just to annoy him."

★ ★ ★

Rushani made a huge fuss when she heard what had happened. She made hot drinks for us and ran a bath for Danny. Then she started telling us off. She said we were never to go on the moors again without an adult.

"See? She does care about you, Danny," I wanted to say.

Will didn't like other people getting all the attention. "Read to me, Mummy," he started whining. "Read me a story."

"Not now, Will. I must make sure Danny is all right. Ask Sophie to read to you."

"I don't want Sophie! I want you to read, Mum!"

"Then you will just have to wait and be patient," she said, and Danny smiled to himself.

In bed that night we talked about what had happened.

"I was terrified," said Danny. "Especially after you disappeared and I was left on my own."

"I was pretty scared too. I don't even believe in God, but I was praying for help."

"Were you? Me too. And then I remembered that verse from the Bible, about God being a rock and a fortress. And I felt a bit better."

"A rock... that's what you need when you're sinking in a swamp," I said.

Twice recently I had prayed to God, first for Will and then for Danny. Twice my prayer had been answered. Did that really mean there was someone out there listening? Or was it all just luck? Maybe I should go along to youth group and find out a bit more.

I said to Danny, "I have some advice for you, next time you get stuck in the bog."

"OK, what should I do?"

"If you're trapped in the bog, don't despair. Just keep banging on the door. In the end someone will come and let you out."

Chapter 15:
Science

On Monday, coming home from school, we noticed a truck coming out of a gateway that led to the woods. It had a phone company logo on the side.

Will was full of excitement. He told us, "They're putting a phone mast on top of the hill! Mum took me up to have a look. It's massive! I wanted to climb up but the men wouldn't let me."

"Don't you ever learn, Will?" Danny groaned. "Do you want to fall on your head again?"

Sophie said, "This could mean I'll be able to use my mobile out here in the sticks." Eagerly she got her phone out to try.

"I don't think the mast is operating yet," said Rushani.

She was right. Sophie, looking fed up, went off to use the computer – *our* computer. Since Sophie moved into the office, no one else had much chance of getting online. She kept saying she needed the computer for homework, but Ben and I were pretty sure she was just chatting to her friends.

Danny asked his mum if we could go to Science Club after school. This meant we would miss the school bus home. Rushani would have to drive into town and pick us up – another problem with living out here. But she didn't mind too much. It was educational.

Mr Martin had put a few posters around the school, with pictures of the mystery substance. *What is this? Animal, vegetable, mineral, or alien? Come to Science Club and help us investigate it!*

Tom Weston had seen the poster. He asked me about it in class.

"That looks like the same stuff that Danny took on the trip. Will he be going to that dumb Science Club? He should fit in all right. It's full of nerds, and Mr Martin is the Chief Nerd."

It didn't sound as if Tom would be going. I felt relieved.

But after school on Thursday, he was in the Chemistry lab, along with a dozen other people. Tom sat down next to Danny and me. Danny immediately got up and moved away.

"Is he still upset about those eggs?" asked Tom. "Some people just can't take a joke, can they?"

I felt awkward. I would have gone to sit with Danny, but I didn't want to annoy Tom. He was in my class; I spent most of the school day with him. And he could be quite mean to people he didn't get on with.

Mr Martin's odd, mismatched eyes were fixed on Tom and me. He didn't look pleased to see us. Earlier that day, he'd got mad at us during a lesson. We had been examining a dead fly under our microscope, instead of the boring slides we were supposed to be looking at. (What was wrong with that? It was still Science, wasn't it?)

"He's keeping an eye on us," I muttered to Tom.

"Yeah, right. Keeping one eye on us while the other one looks somewhere else."

Mr Martin started talking about the blobs of jelly, explaining where he'd found them. He gave us each a few to look at, and asked for suggestions about what they were. There were several ideas, including some that were new to me. Mr Martin wrote them on the board.

"Could it have fallen from a plane? I've read about scientists doing experiments with the weather – trying to seed clouds and make rain."

"Oh, so that's why we've had so much rain in the last few weeks?"

Mr Martin wrote *Rain making* on the board, but then he said, "This substance is not new. I have found references to it in poems written in the 17th century. The poets believed that the jelly came from a falling star – a meteorite, in other words. They did not have planes in those days, of course."

"No, but there might have been alien spaceships," Tom said loudly. "Isn't that right, Danny? Danny's got this theory… these things are the eggs of aliens that are invading the earth."

Danny looked embarrassed. I wished Tom would leave it. But he was clearly enjoying this too much to stop.

"And soon the eggs will hatch out, all over the world. They'll grow into huge alien creatures. Beware! We are all doomed!" He added in a different voice, "That was Danny Fletcher for Sky News, reporting from alien-infested Mallenford."

Everyone laughed. Danny looked as if he wanted to crawl under the bench and hide.

"That is an interesting theory," said Mr Martin. "Is there any evidence to back it up?"

He was looking at Danny, who was speechless with embarrassment. Maybe I should say something about the UFO... but I didn't want Tom to start having a go at me, too.

"I think it's quite likely that aliens exist," said Dylan, a Year 8 boy. "Look how many stars there are – millions of them. Life could have evolved on hundreds of different planets, as well as on earth. Why not?"

"We will not rule out any possibilities," said Mr Martin, writing *Alien Eggs* on the board, underneath *Star Jelly*. "But a scientist always looks for evidence. Any other ideas?"

A girl said, "This jelly – we found a dead frog in our garden, and it had sort of exploded, and you could see white stuff like this inside."

"So aliens are invading our frogs! Will they stop at nothing?" said Tom.

Ignoring him, Mr Martin said, "If a frog contains a substance like this, what is it likely to be?"

"Eggs," said Dylan.

"Yes, unfertilised eggs. The female frog makes large numbers of eggs before hibernating in winter. Then, in spring, she is ready to release them at mating time."

"But there weren't any exploded frogs near this jelly stuff," Danny put in. "It was just lying there by itself."

"I have a theory about that," said Mr Martin. "Many birds, such as herons and birds of prey, eat frogs. But they cannot digest the eggs. So they regurgitate them."

"They do what?" I said.

"He means spew them up," said Tom. "Yuck! I'm not touching that stuff. The insides of a frog, sicked up by a bird!" He pushed the dish of jelly as far away as he could.

"Very well, Tom. You need not touch anything," said Mr Martin. "You may sit and watch our experiments. We shall try to test some of these theories."

He gave out various pieces of equipment and some safety glasses. A couple of people examined the jelly using microscopes. Others measured out chemicals to test the blobs and see what they were made of. This was looking more and more like a science lesson. I began to feel bored.

I wanted to go home, but I'd missed the school bus. I would have to wait until Rushani came to pick us up. Tom, who lived in an outlying village, was trapped here too.

"This is stupid," he said. "But I've had an idea."

"What?"

"Come outside and I'll tell you."

We slipped out of the lab while Mr Martin had his back to us. The school corridor was very quiet, apart from the distant hum of a vacuum cleaner. It was getting dark, and no one had put any lights on in this part of the school.

"Spooky," I said. "It's like the start of a horror movie. All we need is a scary soundtrack and six American teenagers."

"You know what I think?" said Tom. "I think we should set off the fire alarm. That will liven things up a bit in Science Club."

"Tom! Don't be crazy! The last guy who set the alarm off got into big trouble."

"Only because he was an idiot. He did it in daylight, in full view of a CCTV camera. And another mistake… he didn't start an actual fire."

"What? You want to set fire to the school?"

He laughed. "I wouldn't care if the whole place burned down. Would you? But that's not what I was thinking of. We'll just start a *small* fire somewhere. Then nobody will look for the hoaxer who set the alarm off. Because it won't be a hoax."

I stared at him. This was in a different league to the other mad things he'd done. And I didn't want to have anything to do with it.

"Just one little fire. No one will get hurt," he said. "I'd love to start it in the chemistry lab. Then old Martin

107

would get the blame – he must have got careless with his chemicals."

"But the whole place might explode! Anyway, you'd never get away with it. He'd see you."

Tom was silent for a minute, thinking. Then he said, "I'll start things off. I'll set light to a rubbish bin in the cloakroom or somewhere, and hit the fire alarm. Everyone will go outside, just like in a fire drill. Meanwhile we nip back into the lab and start fire number 2. There must be loads of stuff in that lab that would burn."

"No. No! I'm not doing that," I said.

"You're scared," he said scornfully.

"Yeah. Dead right I am. And you're crazy."

"All right then, forget it. I don't need you. I can do this on my own."

The look on his face – excitement and guilt and fear, all mixed up – suddenly reminded me of somebody. Will had looked just like that the other day, when Dad was trying to find his shaving mirror, which had mysteriously vanished.

"You're as bad as my kid brother," I said. "He'd do anything to get noticed."

"Shut up." He looked angry now. "I just said, I don't need you. Go back to the lab and play at doing science with Mr Martin."

"Yes, I think I will."

"But if you say a word to anybody about this, I will kill you, Paul."

I went back. Mr Martin, busy explaining something to one of the groups, didn't notice me at all. I joined Danny and two other boys, who were heating something up in a test tube.

Would Tom actually do anything? I was pretty sure he wouldn't... not on his own. He liked having an audience for his little jokes.

Starting a fire, though -- that wasn't a joke. I wondered if I should say something to Mr Martin. But if I got Tom into trouble, he was certain to pay me back sooner or later.

The minutes ticked away, and nothing happened. I felt relieved. Of course Tom wouldn't really start a fire. He was all talk...

Brrrrrringgggg!

The sound of the fire alarm hammered into my ears, going on and on and on. I'd heard it before at fire drills, of course. But this was not a drill. When someone opened the lab door, a smell of smoke came in.

Oh-oh. He had done it – he'd really done it. Tom had set fire to the school.

Chapter 16:

Health and safety

Calm as anything, Mr Martin made sure we turned off all the equipment. Then he told us to head for the fire assembly point on the playing field. He followed us down to the ground floor and out through a fire exit.

A surprising number of people spilled out of the building which had seemed so empty. Basketball players from the gym. Secretaries and cleaners. The drama group, dressed up like Ancient Romans. Teachers from the staff room, some of them clutching coffee mugs.

It was different from any fire drill I'd ever been to, partly because it was dark outside, partly because everyone was looking nervous. *This isn't a drill. I can smell smoke – where's the fire?*

Out on the dark, windswept field, Mr Martin did a quick head count of the Science Club.

"14," he said. "There were 15 at the start. Who is missing?"

"Tom Weston," said Danny.

"Where is he? I know he is not in the lab because I checked it."

Danny stared at me, as if he thought I would know the answer. I said nothing.

"Maybe he went home early," a girl suggested.

"He couldn't have," said Danny. "He lives in Armlow Green."

"If he went to the toilet, he would still have heard the fire alarm," said Dylan. "Why hasn't he come out?"

"Perhaps he's got locked in," said someone else.

No one looked too worried because, apart from that faint smell of smoke, there was no sign of a fire. From out here, the school seemed quite normal, except for the alarm still sounding like a giant dentist's drill. Lights were on here and there, but not in the lab we'd just left. Its windows were dark.

Where was Tom? What was he doing?

I ought to say something. I ought to tell Mr Martin what Tom had planned to do. But that would get him into bad trouble. At the moment there was nothing to connect him with the fire.

I really didn't want to get on the wrong side of Tom. If I made an enemy of him, he would be sure to get his own back. And he didn't know when to stop – that was the problem.

Come on, Tom! Stop messing about and get out here!

Mrs Grimes, the deputy head, came bustling up to our group. "All present and correct, Leon?" she said to Mr Martin.

"I am afraid I have one boy missing – Tom Weston. I will go in and look for him, with your permission."

"No, you mustn't do that! The fire brigade will be here at any minute. Nobody should go back into the building. Health and safety rules, you know."

Mr Martin was looking uneasy, but he didn't argue. Mrs Grimes hurried off towards the next group of people.

Oh help, God! I don't know what to do. What's the right thing to do here? Keep quiet or speak out?

I knew the answer. But I was afraid to do it.

If I told a teacher, wouldn't I be getting myself into trouble too? I had been in on Tom's plans. I hadn't done anything to stop him. Everyone would be mad at me.

Much safer just to stay quiet, I decided. Stay quiet and hope Tom wouldn't do anything too crazy.

Then Mr Martin said to me, "Paul, you are a friend of Tom's. Do you have any idea where he might be?"

Panicking, I shook my head. "I haven't seen him since we started doing tests on the jelly. He didn't want to join in, remember?"

"So you think he may have left the lab at that point?"

"I don't know! I haven't a clue where he went!"

Again I looked up at the high windows of the lab. But now they weren't quite so dark. I could see the upper walls and ceiling, lit by a pale, flickering light. It looked as if someone had lit a Bunsen burner.

Someone? Tom?

A huge shadow, like some kind of monster, slid across the ceiling. What was Tom doing in there? He didn't know any more science than I did. Set loose in that lab, he was a disaster waiting to happen.

I should say something. I really should… Just give me a minute or two…

Then Danny said to Mr Martin, "I think there's someone in the chemistry lab. I can see a light."

"Maybe that's where Tom is," said Dylan.

Mr Martin didn't waste a moment. "Stay here, all of you," he ordered us. "Nobody must move." Then he ran back towards the school and disappeared inside.

Half a second later a dazzling flash lit the upstairs windows, with a huge bang like a cannon going off. Broken window glass fell tinkling to the ground, and people screamed.

A horrible, choking smell blew towards us on the wind. Inside the lab, flames were leaping up. Was Tom still in there?

"What happened?" Danny gasped. "Did Tom do that?"

"I don't know."

"If he did, he's probably killed himself."

"Where's the fire brigade when you need them?" said one of the other boys.

"They probably think it's another hoax," a girl said.

"Call them again! Somebody do something!"

There was a sick feeling inside me. If only I'd been brave enough to speak out, I might have stopped this from happening. Now it was too late.

Don't say anything or I will kill you… Tom couldn't really have killed me. He could have made my life pretty horrible for a time, but he couldn't have killed me. Had he killed himself?

Then, in the light of the leaping flames, I saw a movement. Someone was coming out of the school... a dark, shadowy figure, bent beneath a heavy load.

"It's Mr Martin! He's got Tom!"

He took a few stumbling steps towards us. Then his knees seemed to give way. He collapsed on the ground, coughing and choking.

We ran towards him. He tried to get up, but couldn't. It sounded as if he was coughing his lungs up.

But Tom looked worse. He lay quite still. I got a glimpse of his face, all blackened. And I had a stupid thought – he wasn't wearing safety glasses. Mr Martin was always very hot on that. But safety glasses couldn't save your life.

"Stand back, everyone!" Mrs Grimes shouted. "Make way for the ambulance!"

The ambulance had arrived along with the fire engine. I remembered the last time I'd seen an ambulance. Thinking of how we'd prayed for Will, I tried to pray again.

But why should God hear me? I had known the right thing to do, but I had refused to do it. It was like I'd turned my back on God. He would never listen to my prayers.

I walked up and down the edge of the field. That bitter, scorching smell was still drifting on the wind. The smoke was invisible in the darkness, but the smell was everywhere.

I had never felt so lonely, so cut off from everyone. What would people say if they knew what I'd done?

The ambulance drove off with its siren blaring. I told myself that Tom must still be alive – otherwise they wouldn't be in such a hurry. Oh, don't let him die!

By the time Rushani came to pick us up, the fire-fighters were starting to put out the flames.

"Can we stay and watch them, Mum?" Will demanded.

Normally I would have been interested too. Quite a crowd had gathered on the playing fields, as people texted and called their friends. *Did you know the school's on fire?*

Now I didn't care. I wanted to go home and wash the smell of smoke off me. I wanted to forget the whole thing. But I couldn't.

Chapter 17:
A new beginning

In assembly the next day, the head talked to the whole school about what had happened. I was relieved to hear that Tom was alive.

"But he is still in a coma," said the head, "and the doctors don't know if he will come out of it. Even if he does, his eyesight may be permanently damaged. Or his brain."

"So, no change there then," I heard someone say. Other people told him to shut up.

"Mr Martin very bravely went into the burning school to bring Tom out. He's in hospital too, suffering from the effects of smoke. I need not tell you what an extremely foolish thing it was that Tom Weston did…"

But he did tell us, several times over, until we were all sick of hearing it.

Passing the locked chemistry lab, you could still smell smoke. From outside the building, you could see the blown-out windows, and the walls blackened by fire. It looked like something in a war zone.

Time after time I was forced to remember that night. I saw again the bright, blinding flash which might be the last thing Tom could ever see. And I wished, over and over, that I had spoken out while there was still time. I should have been braver… but it was too late now.

★ ★ ★

That weekend there was a phone call from Mum. She still rang us every couple of weeks. But it was more than two years since she left, and nowadays it felt more like talking to a stranger than to your own mother.

I didn't want to talk to her. I knew I wouldn't be able to make myself sound like I was happy, doing well and getting on with my life – which was what Mum wanted to hear.

"Tell her I'm busy," I said to Ben. "I don't want to talk right now."

When Ben put the phone down, he said, "She's upset because you wouldn't talk to her."

"Tough," I said. "Not as upset as we were when she left, I bet."

"She's thinking of coming back at Christmas for a couple of weeks."

"Just Mum?" I said.

"No, both of them. Mum and Mike. I suppose he wants to see his kids, too."

Once, I would have leapt at the thought of seeing Mum again. I would have secretly started hoping that she would come back for good. But now I didn't know what to think.

Did I actually want to see her? It would just complicate things. And life was complicated enough already.

★ ★ ★

On Sunday evening I went to youth group with Danny. Even there, I couldn't forget what had happened to Tom, because the youth leader prayed for him. By now he had been in a coma for three days.

"Is he going to get better?" one of the girls asked.

"We don't know," said Joe. "We must keep praying for him."

Joe's talk that night was about David. Many years after the fight with Goliath, David became king. He fell in love with a woman called Bathsheba, who was married to a soldier in David's army. They had an affair while the husband, Uriah, was away at the war. When Uriah began to suspect what was going on, David decided to get rid of him.

"David sent a secret message to the commander of the army. Uriah was to be put in the front line of the next battle. When enemies surrounded him, David's army was to pull back and leave him to be killed. In other words, David arranged for the murder of this man, who hadn't done anything wrong, so that he could steal his wife."

"That's terrible," said one of the girls.

Danny said, "I thought David was supposed to be a hero."

"Even heroes, even good people, are never perfect," said Joe. "Every one of us does things that are against God's laws. Hating people. Stealing. Telling lies. Cheating on people. And when we do that, bad things follow like night follows day.

"Not long after that, David and Bathsheba had a baby son. The baby got very ill. David prayed for him for seven days and nights, hoping God would heal him. But God didn't answer his prayer... The baby died. You see, the worst thing that happens when we do wrong is this: we get cut off from God. We get separated from him. We can't talk to him. We can't hear his voice."

"Kind of unfair that the baby died," said somebody. "He didn't do anything bad, did he?"

"But that's what happens when people start doing wrong," said Joe. "Evil spreads out like smoke from a bonfire, and other people are affected by it. One cruel leader causes thousands of innocent deaths. Greedy businessmen start a credit crunch, and hundreds of people are made homeless. Parents cheat on each other and split up, and their children get hurt. That's what our world is like.

"Don't get me wrong – this isn't how God wanted the world to be. He created it to be perfect. But people decided to go their own way, rather than God's way, and evil got more and more powerful."

"So why doesn't God do something about it?" I asked.

Joe said, "He already has. He sent Jesus, his own son, into this messed-up world where evil fights against good. Someone totally good, someone strong, brave and perfect, came to live on earth. And what happened?"

"People hated him," said a girl. "They killed him."

"Yes. Jesus knew that would happen – he warned his friends beforehand. Like the teacher who rescued Tom, the only way he could save us was by going into danger himself. He went through a terrible, slow, agonising death. He cried out to God, *Why have you forsaken me?* And then he died. It must have seemed as if evil had won in the end."

"But then God brought him to life again," someone said.

"Yes, and his death made a way for all of us to come back to God. Whatever we have done in our lives, God will forgive us, if we ask him. In the words of David's own prayer:

I have sinned against you and done evil in your sight...
Cleanse me, and I shall be clean;
wash me and I shall be whiter than snow...
Create in me a pure heart, O God."

I liked the sound of those words. I wished Joe would read them again.

"None of us will ever be perfect while we live on earth," said Joe. "But when we do something bad, we can always turn back to God and ask him to forgive us. And he will help us to live the way he wants – on the side of good, not evil. We can know him. He'll be our rock and our fortress."

Once again he read the words that David wrote, and I echoed them inside my head. *I'm sorry, God. Sorry I didn't obey you.*

A lot of other things came into my mind – things I'd done that I knew were wrong. Being mean to Danny. Not always telling the truth. Getting mad at Will. Refusing to talk to Mum when she rang.

I have sinned against you and done evil in your sight… cleanse me, and I shall be clean.

The weird thing was, I did feel different when I'd prayed. I felt better somehow. All new and fresh, like it was New Year's Day, the start of a different year where nothing had gone wrong… yet.

I looked up and saw Danny's face. I was pretty sure he had just done the same thing as I had. He'd prayed that prayer and really meant it.

Will you truly forgive us and change us, God? Can we really know you? Will you be our rock and our fortress?

My mind was full of questions. But only one answer came back to me… *Wait and see.*

Chapter 18:
A hero

A few days later, there was better news about Tom. He'd come out of the coma; he was able to see and speak all right. But his face and hands had been quite badly burned. He wouldn't be back in school for some time.

Mr Martin was back, though. He looked no different from before – a small, grey-haired man, not at all like a hero. In movies, the usual hero is a fit young guy with a strange resemblance to a famous film star. Mr Martin would only have been filmed as an extra in a crowd scene. But in real life he was a hero all right.

In assembly, the head made him go up on the stage while everyone clapped. He looked quite embarrassed. The head thanked him for helping to save Tom's life. Then Mr Martin warned everyone about taking risks in a science lab.

"A laboratory is a dangerous place. When I was a student, I made a careless mistake, which caused an explosion. In those days people did not use safety glasses. I lost one eye. I was fortunate not to be blind for the rest of my life."

So that was the reason his eyes seemed to look in different directions – one of them was a fake. (Which one? It might be useful to know.)

People listened more to what Mr Martin said than to the head's lecture a few days earlier. After all, Mr Martin had been through it himself. He knew what he was talking about.

A couple of weeks went by. Not long now to the end of term, which was good, because school was pretty boring without Tom around. I had nobody to mess about with in lessons.

But this meant that I didn't get into so much trouble with teachers. And I began to notice something... My reading seemed slightly better than it used to be. Maybe all that reading practice with Rushani was actually helping.

Things at home were going all right. The extension was coming on well, all wired up and plumbed in. Now the painters were at work. Sophie had decided to have a pink bedroom; Danny wanted a black ceiling with fluorescent stars; Will had chosen a Thomas the Tank Engine theme which he would probably hate in a year or two.

Danny and I were really making an effort to get on with people. We had a secret *Be nice to Will* week and a *Stop Sophie arguing* agreement. (After a while Sophie guessed what we were doing, and if we tried to calm things down, she argued worse than ever.)

Ben was much less moody now that he was back in his own room. Sophie was happier because the new phone mast was operating, and she could call her friends as much as she liked.

In fact, it was all so smooth and peaceful that Dad and Rushani decided they could leave us alone for one night. Dad's company was having a special Christmas do because it was their 50th anniversary. There would be a posh meal, a dance band and an entertainer. It wouldn't finish until the early hours of the morning. Sophie and Ben would be left in charge of the house.

Rushani looked amazing in a gold-embroidered sari, like an Indian movie star. Dad, in a hired dinner jacket, didn't look too bad for once. I hoped they would have a nice evening.

"Are you sure you will be all right?" Rushani said to Ben and Sophie.

"Mum, we're nearly 16. We'll be fine," said Sophie.

Ben said, "And if we need you, we can ring you at the hotel."

"Go on, Mum. Have a great time and don't worry," Sophie said. "What could possibly go wrong?"

Things that could possibly go wrong:
1 Sophie inviting all her friends around for a party. (Maybe it was a good thing we lived out in the sticks.)
2 Will being sick.
3 Will wetting the bed.
4 Will having a screaming fit and wanting his mum.
5 Ben trying to boss Danny around, e.g. telling him when to go to bed.
6 Danny refusing to do it, a fight starting, somebody getting hurt.
7 The house being burgled.
8 The house catching fire.

9   The house being flooded by a burst pipe.
(If 8 and 9 both happened, they might cancel each other out. But I thought the odds were rather against that.)

Later in the evening, Danny asked me to help him set up his telescope outside. It was a clear night, and he wanted to look at the Pleiades, whatever that meant.

We carried the telescope and tripod downstairs and set it up on the back lawn, halfway between the house and the woods. The chilly night air made me shiver.

"Why don't you set up your telescope in the new attic?" I asked him.

"The windows aren't facing the right way. Anyway, it's just as cold in there as out here."

Sophie came out to see what was happening. "Did Mum say you could do this?"

"She didn't say I couldn't," Danny said evasively.

"Yeah, because you didn't ask her. I know you."

"She wouldn't mind," I said. "There's no school tomorrow, remember? It's Saturday."

Sophie must have been in a good mood. "OK. Just make sure you don't freeze to death," she said, and went back indoors.

Danny said, "I love the sky out here. You can see far more stars than in town. No light pollution from street lights and things."

He found the Pleiades with his telescope and let me have a look. I saw a group of bluish-white stars, clear and bright.

"They're young stars," said Danny.

"How do you know?"

"By the colour. Look at Betelgeuse – that's much older." He readjusted the telescope and showed me a bigger star with an orange tinge to it.

"It's 640 light years away from earth. That's trillions of miles. The light we're seeing left Betelgeuse in 1300-and-something. Maybe the star doesn't even exist any more, but we won't know that for hundreds of years."

"What could happen to it?" I asked.

"It could go supernova and explode, and kill us all with gamma radiation," he said cheerfully.

"Do you really think that might happen?"

"I used to. But now I don't. For some reason God cares about our tiny little planet. Even though he made all that... all those millions of stars..."

He ran out of words, gazing up at the sky.

The stars were beautiful, but so far away. Was it really true that God, who made them, could come close to us... could care about each one of us?

Danny showed me a few more stars through his telescope, but after a while I got cold. I went indoors and watched a DVD with Ben and Sophie. Will, who was supposed to be in bed, kept on coming downstairs, but Sophie was quite strict with him. She told him off and took him back upstairs.

"Why is Danny allowed outside in the dark and not me? It's so unfair!" I heard him moaning.

"When you're as old as Danny, you'll be allowed to do what he's doing," said Sophie. "If you're crazy enough to want to."

After a while, even Danny got tired of the cold, and came indoors to get warmed up. He went back out again later, but I was sleepy. I took myself off to bed.

I don't know why I woke up. It wasn't Danny's snoring this time, because the light from the landing showed his bed still empty. My clock said 2:15.

Was Danny all right? Surely he wasn't still outside?

I went to the window. The lawn was white with frost. I could see the dark outline of the telescope, but Danny wasn't there. He must have come indoors again.

Then I saw that Will's bed was empty too. I wondered if he'd crept downstairs, wanting to be outside like his big brother. I'd better make sure he was OK.

I went down into the hall, and found that the back door was wide open. Will and Danny were nowhere to be seen.

The house was very quiet. The downstairs lights were off. Sophie and Ben must have gone to bed... or had they disappeared too? A cold fear clutched at my heart.

Where had everyone gone? Had they all been kidnapped, or abducted by aliens? Was I the only one left?

Chapter 19:

Vanished

I ran outside. The frost was as sharp as needles under my bare feet. In the cold, still air, nothing moved.

There was absolutely no sign of anyone. Oh, God, help! What's happened? What do I do now?

Don't panic. Go and look for Ben.

Racing upstairs, I flung open Ben's bedroom door. I had never, ever been so pleased to see my brother lying asleep in his own bed.

"Ben. Ben! Wake up!"

"Wha'ssa matter?" he said sleepily.

"Will and Danny have disappeared! The back door was wide open. I don't know where they've gone!"

Instantly he was awake. We went to make sure Sophie was all right, and then the three of us went through the whole house, old rooms and new. Danny and Will were nowhere to be found.

Will might possibly hide from us, just to be annoying. Not Danny, though. And another thing – the telescope. Danny wouldn't have left it out there unless something had happened.

But what? What was going on?

"I'll ring Mum," said Sophie. But she couldn't get a signal on her phone.

"Use the house phone," said Ben. "I'll go and have a look outside."

"I'll come too," I said.

"Not like that you won't," he said. Realising that I was still in pyjamas, I hurried to get a coat and some shoes.

We went out into the back garden. Ben shone a torch around.

"Hey! Look at this!"

When he shone the torch on the ground, I could see footprints in the frosty grass – little, elf-like ones that could only be from Will's slippers. And Danny's footmarks were all around the telescope.

Then we saw a line of prints leading towards the woods... a double line, from Danny's feet and Will's. Had Will run off, and Danny chased him?

Ben looked carefully at the footprints. "I'd say Danny went first, and Will followed him."

"Maybe Danny didn't know Will was behind him," I said.

"But why did he go off into the woods in the middle of the night?"

I could only think of one reason. "He could have been spying on the stranger in the woods. He must have seen the light we saw a few weeks ago."

Ben looked worried. "Why didn't he come and tell us?"

"Sophie would have made him stay indoors," I said. "And you know Danny. He likes finding out about things."

"That boy is an idiot," Ben said savagely.

We followed the footprints as far as we could, into the fringes of the wood. There was hardly any frost in the shelter of the trees, and no more prints.

It was very dark in the wood. Dark branches hung over us. Dark leaves covered the ground in a slimy layer. The torch created more shadows than light, and the shadows shifted eerily whenever we moved.

I longed to go back home, lock the doors and put all the lights on. I was starting to feel really scared.

We went on a little further through the trees, with no idea which way to go. I shouted Danny's name. My voice sounded small and thin in the vast, cold, empty night.

"Danny! Will! Are you there?" Ben's voice was no stronger than mine – he was scared too, I suddenly realised.

Nobody answered. The silence of the forest swallowed up all sounds.

"They could be anywhere," Ben muttered. "How are we supposed to find them?"

"Do you think we should go back?"

I wanted him to say yes. I wanted to go home and wait for Dad to come. I would feel so much braver, so much safer, if Dad was here.

Then I remembered something. *You are my rock and my fortress...*

Oh God, help me! Be my rock, be my fortress. Give me courage like David's, to face the giants of fear and darkness.

And suddenly I knew that God was with me, even here. God, who made darkness and light, was all around me, closer than the air I breathed. I felt his strength and courage flowing into me.

I took a deep breath. "I think we should keep on looking."

"All right. I'll give it five more minutes," said Ben. "Then I'm going back."

We went up the hill, shouting for Will and Danny. And then, at last, I heard something. Hurrying footsteps scuttered through the trees. The torchlight shone on a small figure in a blue dressing-gown.

"Will! Over here!"

He ran down the hill towards us. I'd never seen him look so scared – he could hardly speak.

"There's a UFO," he gasped. "A spaceship. It hit the phone mast!"

"What?"

"Where's Danny?" I asked.

"I don't know. I think the aliens got him!" And he started to tremble.

"Will. Will! Calm down for a minute. Tell us what happened," said Ben.

He said shakily, "I saw a UFO. A big black thing. I saw it from the window. Danny ran after it, into the woods…"

"And you ran after Danny," I said.

"Yes, but I couldn't find him. He'd gone. I went right up the hill. I saw the UFO stuck on the phone mast, and I saw an alien with no face!"

We stared at him. This couldn't really be happening. He must be remembering a bad dream.

I put my arms around him, trying to warm him up. He hid his face against me, like a small, scared animal.

"I tried to go home but I got lost," he whispered. "I was so frightened… and then I heard you shouting my name."

"You're all right now. There aren't any aliens here," said Ben, shining the torch all around.

"Don't do that! They'll see us!" Will said, sounding terrified. "Where's Mum? I want my mum!"

"All right," I said. "Don't cry, Will. Mum and Dad will be back soon. It's going to be OK."

Each of us took one of his hands, and we hurried down the hill. He was shivering with cold and fear. Even when we got him indoors, into the warmth, he was still shaking. Sophie wrapped him up in a blanket and held him on her knee. He started to cry.

"Mum! I want Mum!"

"She's on her way back right now," said Sophie.

"How long?" I asked.

"Half an hour, they said."

Half an hour. We could stay indoors and wait for Dad to come back... or we could go out again and look for Danny.

I really didn't want to go out again. Too many weird things were happening. This was the scariest night of my life. *I saw an alien with no face... I think the aliens got him...*

But some of that strange courage was still warming me up from the inside, making me feel strong. I knew that God was still with me, here at home or out in the dark wood.

"I'm going out to look for Danny," I said.

"No," said Ben. "We should wait for Dad. That's the safest thing to do."

Sophie looked from me to Ben, then back to me again.

"I'll come with you," she said. "Ben, can you look after Will?"

She tried to stand up. But Will clutched at her and started screaming.

"I'll go," Ben said hastily. "You stay with Will."

"When Dad comes, tell him we went up the hill towards the new phone mast," I said. "Will was babbling on about it. If Danny saw the same thing as Will, that's where he'll be."

"After we've gone out, lock the door," said Ben.

We went up the hill as quietly as we could. Ben still had the torch, but he didn't shine it around like before. He kept it aimed at the ground in front of us, shielding it with his hand.

A small, winding path brought us out on the upper side of the wood. I looked for the new phone mast on the hilltop. And then I gasped.

Something huge and dark was blotting out half the stars. It was too round and smooth to be a cloud. Three lights shone out from the underside.

"The UFO," I whispered.

The thing wasn't moving, and I saw that Will was right. Somehow it had snagged itself on the phone mast. I could hear a low, snake-like hissing sound, like gas escaping.

So Will hadn't been dreaming about the UFO. What if he had really seen an alien?

And still there was no sign of Danny. I didn't dare to call out his name – not here, so close to the Thing.

That ominous hissing grew louder. I never heard any sound of movement from behind. But all at once I felt a touch on my shoulder. I knew it wasn't Ben, for he was in front of me.

Automatically I looked down. It wasn't a hand… or not a human hand. It was grey. It felt tough and smooth and leathery against my neck.

I wanted to scream, but no sound came out. Very, very slowly, I turned around.

Chapter 20:

So far away

The creature was as tall as a man, but dark grey all over. And it didn't seem to have a face – only darkness, with two white eyes staring out.

Instantly those eyes took in the terror on my face.

"Don't be scared, lad, I won't eat you," it said.

It spoke English! Amazing!

"Who... who are you?" I whispered.

"The name's John. Who are you?"

Suddenly I heard Danny's voice from close at hand. "These are my brothers – Paul and Ben."

Ben swung around and shone the torch first at Danny, then at the tall figure beside him. And I saw what it really was. Not an alien at all – an ordinary man in motorbike leathers, with a black balaclava covering most of his face.

I felt totally stupid. Luckily I hadn't said anything too crazy-sounding, like *Welcome to our planet. Do you come in peace?*

Danny said, "You know that den we found in the woods – this is the guy who made it. He's been keeping watch, trying to find out more about that thing." He pointed towards the UFO.

"What is it?" asked Ben.

"Some kind of airship," said John. "They've been developing it at the air base. It seems to be unmanned – they must be directing it by remote control."

"What for?" I said.

"We think it might be used to carry an E-bomb. Do you know what that is? It's the latest idea in war weapons. It doesn't kill people, it kills machines. It sends out a massive burst of electromagnetic radiation. Computers and phones and household wiring – all kinds of electrical things – are ruined. Most vehicles are immobilised. Life as we know it grinds to a halt."

"I suppose it's less cruel than blowing people up," I said.

"It doesn't kill people straight away, that's true," he said. "But think of the impact on a city. No power supply, no water, no transport. No food in the shops. People would soon be dying from hunger and thirst and disease."

"Wait a minute. Are you a spy?" Ben asked him. "Who are you working for?"

"For the whole world," he said grandly. "I belong to the PPPG... the Peaceful Planet Pressure Group. Ever heard of it? We believe that governments – all governments – should cut down their spending on weapons research. There are far better uses for the money. They've probably wasted millions developing this thing, and look at it! It can't even fly properly!"

"Something must have gone wrong with it," said Danny. "When I saw it from the garden, it was flying so low it nearly hit our chimneys. I thought it was an alien spaceship coming in to land."

"So you followed it, like an idiot," said Ben.

"And Will followed you," I said. "Didn't you realise?"

"Oh, no!" Danny looked suddenly worried. "Where is he?"

"It's all right. We found him. He's safe at home now."

Suddenly John held up his hand. "Listen! Here they come!"

"Who?"

"The military. Come to look for their new toy."

I could hear the sound of a helicopter coming rapidly closer.

"Keep back. Keep out of sight," said John. "I'm going to try and take some photos. But if this lot find me, they'll seize my camera. I might even get arrested."

He lay down in the cover of some bushes. The rest of us moved further back into the wood. Ben switched the torch off, and we waited silently.

Two helicopters landed beyond the trees, and men spilled out of them. A bright searchlight was aimed up at the airship thing. For the first and only time, I got a proper look at it.

It was black all over, with a strange sheen to it. The main body was oval-shaped. A much smaller cube-shape hung down below, and this was the part that had caught on the mast.

I'd seen a TV programme about stealth planes which were undetectable to radar. Maybe this was similar. Flying low, this thing could slip across a border under cover of darkness, travelling silently to its destination. Then it could set off an E-bomb that would cripple a whole city. Its own controls would be destroyed too, but that wouldn't matter. It would have done its work.

John crept back towards us. "I got some good pictures," he whispered. "Look out for them on our website. I'm off now, before they decide to search the area. You'd be wise to go too."

Danny didn't want to leave, but Ben and I dragged him away. We thought Dad might already be setting out to look for us, or even calling the police.

We hurried down the hill. Our car was coming up the drive, far too fast, bumping over the potholes.

As Dad and Rushani got out, all five of us surrounded them. We were all talking at once. I could see Dad checking that everybody was there. Rushani held her arms out, as if she wanted to hug all of us at once.

And a strange thought came to me... It felt as if we were a family at last.

★ ★ ★

In the morning, we looked for John's photos on the Internet. They were there all right on the PPPG website. But not for long.

The next time we looked, we got the message, *The page cannot be found.* In fact the whole website seemed to have disappeared.

"They're trying to cover everything up," said Ben.

"They?" said Danny. "Who?"

"The government. The military."

But it was too late for a cover-up. The pictures appeared again on other sites. Questions were asked in parliament. Newspapers demanded to know why taxpayers' money was being wasted. (*Million-pound balloon – where's the party?*)

"This would make a good story, if we could write it down," I said to Danny. "Better than your made-up one about purple mind-reading aliens."

"Write it, then," he said.

"You know I'm no good at spelling and writing and stuff."

"I'll help. We'll write it together."

There wasn't time to start straight away, though. We were too busy organising the move into the new part of the house. At last I was able to get my own bedroom back and be as untidy as I liked. I set up my drum kit in the attic, with several layers of old carpet under it. (But Sophie still moaned about the noise coming through her ceiling.)

The attic room was great. Ben and Sophie were already planning to have a shared birthday party there, and arguing about who to invite. The whole house was pretty good, in fact. We couldn't believe how much space we had, after being cramped together for so long.

I helped Will to move his things to his new bedroom. There was a shoebox he wouldn't let me touch. He said it had secret things in it... Christmas secret things. But as he tried to squeeze it under his bed, the box broke, and something slid out.

A phone? Will had a plastic toy phone, but this looked like a real one. Wait a minute – it looked like my phone, the one that had disappeared ages ago.

"Will! This is mine! You stole it!"

"I never," he said. "I found it under the sofa."

"Why didn't you tell me? You knew I was looking for it."

"Because I didn't like you very much then. But I do now. I'm going to give you the phone for Christmas."

"You can't give people their own things as a present! What else have you got in there?"

There was quite a collection.

– Dad's lost shaving mirror.
– Two DVDs belonging to Ben.
– Rushani's favourite earrings.
– A bright pink lipstick (Sophie's, obviously).
– A half-eaten packet of biscuits.
– A tattered-looking *Thomas the Tank Engine* book.

"Who are the book and the biscuits for?" I asked. "You?"

He nodded. I had to laugh.

"Don't tell anybody, will you?" he pleaded. "It's a Christmas surprise."

"OK."

But there was a much bigger surprise in store. Rushani and Dad called us all together. They said they had something to tell us.

"We are expecting a baby," Rushani said.

There was a moment's silence. Nobody knew quite what to say. *Aren't five kids enough for you?* was the first thing that came to mind.

But Dad and Rushani were looking so happy. He held her hand, and she smiled up at him. It seemed a shame to spoil the moment.

"That's really great, Mum!" said Sophie.

"Yeah, congratulations," I said, and everyone else joined in.

"We should have made another bedroom in that extension, shouldn't we?" said Dad.

"The baby can share my room," Will said generously. "If it's a boy, that is. I'm not sharing with a girl."

Danny gave him a pitying look. And I remembered what he'd said about his feelings when Will arrived. A baby taking over the house, invading his space... Will didn't know what he was in for.

★ ★ ★

I was helping Rushani to make a Sri Lanka-style Christmas cake. As well as all the usual stuff, it had pumpkin and ginger preserve in it, and rose essence, and something mysterious called chow-chow (a kind of pickle). The mixture smelled wonderful.

In the middle of this, the phone rang.

It was Mum, with some bad news. Mike had fallen and broken his leg – they wouldn't be able to come over for Christmas after all. They would try to come and see us in the spring, when he was better.

I didn't know whether to feel sorry or relieved. Now we could have our first Christmas together as a family, just the seven of us. It was likely to be quite problematic already, without having to think about sharing the time with Mum and Mike.

"Paul, I'm really sorry we won't be able to make it. I was looking forward to seeing you again. Phone calls aren't much use, are they? Every time I put the phone down, I feel... oh, I don't know." Mum's voice sounded lonely and sad. "I just wish we weren't so far away."

Well, you're the one who chose to go, I felt like saying. But I bit back the words. I wondered what kind of a Christmas Mum and Mike would have, all by themselves. A quiet, civilised, boring one, I guessed.

"I'm sorry we won't be seeing you, too," I said. "We'll call you on Christmas Day."

Our Christmas was likely to be the total opposite of Mum and Mike's... noisy, uncivilised, far from boring. We had two different lots of family traditions to argue about.

– Hanging up stockings/pillowcases.
– Going to church/staying at home in the warm.
– Opening presents at midnight/after breakfast.

- Fighting for control of the PlayStation/Wii.
- Eating roast turkey and potatoes/chicken cashew nut curry and yellow rice.
- Arguing over Monopoly/Scalextric.
- Feeling ill after too much spicy food/too many sweets.
- Falling asleep in front of the Queen's Speech/*The Great Escape*.
- Keeping the house tidy/living in a mess until the New Year.

Somehow, though, we all ended up going to the late night carol service on Christmas Eve. Even Ben and Sophie decided at the last minute to come along.

I sat in church, listening to the old story being read from the Bible – the story of God's Son being born on earth. I never used to believe it really. It was just a story, something that was brought out at Christmas along with the glitter and lights, and put away again soon after.

But it actually happened. Instead of being far away, higher than the stars, God's Son came to earth as a human child. Far more amazing than any alien invasion, good invaded evil. God's power invaded people's lives and changed them for ever.

And it's still happening. Two thousand years later, God is still ready to come into our lives. To speak to us. To be our rock and fortress.

★ ★ ★

After the service, a friend of Rushani's came over to talk to us. "Lovely to see your whole family in church," she said.

Rushani smiled at the five of us. Dad said, "It's Christmas. Peace on earth, goodwill to all men, and no arguments. Amazing! But I don't suppose it will last."

He was right. Before we got home, Sophie was moaning about something, Danny and Ben were quarrelling, and Will was demanding to stay up until Santa came. *Happy Christmas, everyone*, I felt like saying.

We got out of the car into the silence of the night. There was a clear sky, and the stars were wonderfully bright.

"Oh look, a shooting star!" said Sophie. "Did you see it, Will? Make a wish."

Gazing upwards, I made a few wishes myself. I wished for peace on earth and throughout the whole universe, goodwill to all men and alien life-forms, and no more arguments or wars. Was that too much to ask for?

"Come on, let's go inside," Rushani said, shivering.

And we all went into our home and shut the door.